KICK THE ANIMAL OUT

by Véronique Ovaldé

TRANSLATED BY ADRIANA HUNTER

KICK THE ANIMAL OUT

by Véronique Ovaldé

TRANSLATED BY ADRIANA HUNTER

MACADAM CAGE

MacAdam Cage
155 Sansome Street, Suite 550
San Francisco, CA 94104
www.macadamcage.com

Library of Congress Cataloging-in-Publication Data

Ovaldé, Véronique, 1972-

  [Déloger l'animal. English]

  Kick the animal out / by Véronique Ovaldé ; translated by Adriana Hunter.

      p. cm.

  ISBN 978-1-59692-202-0 (alk. paper)

  I. Hunter, Adriana. II. Title.

PQ2675.V35D4513 2007

843'.92—dc22

                                    2006103271

Paperback edition: April, 2007

ISBN 978-1-59692-202-0

Manufactured in the United States of America

10 9 8 7 6 5 4 3 2 1

Book and jacket design by Dorothy Carico Smith

Cet ouvrage, publié dans le cadre d'un programme d'aide à la publication, bénéficie du soutien financier du Ministère des affaires Etrangères et
du Service Culturel de l'Ambassade de France aux Etats-Unis, ainsi que de
l'appui du French American Cultural Exchange.

This work, published as part of a program providing publication assis-
tance, received financial support from the Cultural Services of the French
Embassy in the United States and the French American Cultural Exchange.
www.frenchbooknews.com

PREFACE

As a child, Véronique Ovaldé, like so many other writers, fled to the library where books came to occupy a passionate role in her inner life. They became not only vehicles of escape from what felt like a drab existence in the housing projects outside her hometown of Paris, but "manuals of insubordination," in which she discovered the multiple languages she needed to burst the constrictions of personal and literary isolation. Her voracious reading laid the groundwork for the novelist's plurality, the multi-voiced chamber of narrative fiction, which she describes as "a slipping and sliding." It is this shuddering motion that informs her style and gives it both flexibility and originality.

Ovaldé's *Kick the Animal Out* travels back and forth from the always robust and at times hallucinatory inner landscape of a girl's mind to the pedestrian realities of her everyday existence. The threshold between the two, however, is not fixed, but fluid. The internal colors the external, and the external colors the internal in a text that masterfully combines these two realms of human experience. At the book's heart is a single mystery: the sudden, unexplained disappearance of Rose's mother. This absence creates an emotional urgency that drives the story forward as the daughter tries to make sense of what has happened to her from the fragments of information she gathers over time. With each of Rose's conversations, memories, imaginings, and speculations, Ovaldé's narrative deepens and grows more poignant. Along with Rose, the reader begins to piece together the painful story of the missing mother. But more than anything perhaps, the novel vividly portrays the psychic tumult of a child faced with a terrible loss. It is a testament to Ovaldé's gifts as a prose writer that the portrait she gives us is very funny and very sad, refined and stark, highly idiosyncratic, and yet finally, universal.

Siri Hustvedt

KICK THE ANIMAL OUT

ONE

I LOOKED AT HER SLUMPED IN HER CHAIR, her eyes vacant, glued to the TV screen. She couldn't drum up any enthusiasm for the pointless electrical items they were trying to persuade her to buy at sacrificial prices (better tighten our belts), and at irresponsible prices (better forget we ever wanted to improve our souls). I'm sure she was only looking at her own reflection on the screen, stunned by her own inertia, occasionally twitching the fingers of her right hand to check that she could still move. There she stayed, with her ankles crossed on the cushion—the one with masses of little mirrors sewn onto it that Mr. Loyal had bought her, an airport souvenir folded a dozen times to fit into his suitcase on wheels, the cursing sweating effort of making it small enough so he could bring his wife a present, a kind thought, an almost nothing, an "I thought of you on the last day before mailing the postcards."

I was standing in the doorway. I adjusted the

fastening on the cape around my neck, draped its black silk over me—the fuchsia pink lining was not overly discreet but it was all I could find, a vampire outfit, I hadn't wanted the teeth even though they were pretty striking, I just wanted this black cape with the pink lining so that I could fly away more easily, I just wanted a silk cape I could wrap around myself when my mother had that dead face and those lost, almost transparent yellow eyes.

I draped my black silk cape with the fuchsia lining around me, opened the window, climbed onto the sill and—without taking a last look at my lovely, wasted mother—I threw myself into the air.

PART ONE

TWO

WHEN ROSE MET MY FATHER—my kind father, the circus manager—when Rose met her Mr. Loyal, she was already pregnant with me.

But her stomach was so flat—her magnificent hipbones created a sort of basin between them—her stomach was so flat that my father didn't suspect I was there. After a little time, he put his hands onto her hipbones and told her, you have such a long flat stomach, it's the stomach of a sterile little girl...My father, Mr. Loyal, can't have said anything like that. My mother told me what he said but I just can't believe he could have uttered a sentence like that, he was the sort of man who had no malice in him, the sort of man who never gave things infinite meaning, he was like a pocket mirror, a practical thing with a red leatherette case that you could pop in your purse, a world away from those medicine cabinets where you can angle the mirrored doors opposite each other and watch the infiniteness of it all.

She would say, he talked about my sterile little girl's stomach, and then start laughing, her eyes shining, can you imagine?

I could imagine.

And I felt just a little bit hurt, because of that very flat stomach that had tricked my father's judgment.

But my mother wasn't laughing to make fun of him, she was amazed he could be so innocent, delighted that her circus manager was so naïve. Can you imagine, can you imagine? she kept saying. (Mom often repeated things three times. These triplets set a rhythm to her conversations like some mysterious regulation.)

I never answered, I would get up from my chair, smooth my cape, and say with a sigh, I'm going to the bathroom or I'm getting a cookie. And I would go and look for a packet of cookies in the sideboard, and make a lot of noise opening it, ripping and stripping the cardboard, tearing and scattering the plastic packaging all over the tiled floor. Then squirrel-like nibbling, choking, and related noises. She understood why I was making all this racket—showers of crumbs on the Formica, swallowing, lemonade glug-glugging into the glass and fizzing in my throat, microsound of explosions, multiplication and pulverization—so she would say, sorry, sorry, sorry, and smile at me, adding, anyway, I adore your father. And when she said this I never knew which father she was talking about, the circus manager or the one who had deposited me with his dick in the depths of my mother's body—and I imagined he had deposited dozens of other children in women's bellies, I could have been a black boy in a pitch-black belly, that's what I imagined on the subject of my other father (the one who wasn't a circus manager), I imagined him specializing in impregnating girls.

That gave me something to think about.

THREE

WHEN MY FATHER MET ROSE, my father, the real one, the one with the dick, she was devastatingly pretty. He was the only one who realized it. When he saw her he felt like he'd stumbled across something gleaming at the bottom of a cave, something fluttering like a little bird's heart. He watched my mother walk past, he watched her going backward and forward in the schoolyard—should he see some sort of invitation in the repetition of this trip or was it actually just the natural mechanics of the muscles in my mother's thighs and calves working in tune with her thoughts, and absolutely unconnected to the boy standing in the covered yard, a boy who was so young and arrogant that he was invisible, but conscious—now that he was confronted with the princely indifference of my mother, who was not yet my mother—of his own youth and arrogance.

Her clothes were secondhand and altered to fit but they still had a trace of their previous shape, faithful as a mattress keeping the imprint of a body. He felt his heart break and he felt clammy, that's what he thought, fuck, my heart's breaking and I feel clammy, but he kept on waiting under the covered yard, rolling his cigarettes, he could roll them so perfectly that he sold them under the chestnut trees.

My future father didn't go to see her right away. He waited for several weeks. He just wanted to watch her walk past. He wondered how she managed to be so attractive when she wasn't wearing the red All Stars everyone was supposed to wear, when she didn't have the plastic khaki sports bag that all the girls had to have, when she didn't chat to any of the other girls about pop music and the "bests" (prettiest girls, coolest ski resorts, hippest radio stations: everything could be cataloged), my father looked at her and asked himself questions—which gave him a foretaste of unsuspected abysses in his own depths. He felt trapped and that made him nervous, he felt like a space probe sent hurtling thousands of light-years into the most terrifying darkness, a probe that might pass right next to my mother but would be incapable of stopping its own headlong flight toward death. My father was worried about having thoughts like this, he tried everything he could to flatten himself on the ground with his face in the grass, to try and stop thinking of this girl as anything more than badly dressed and

slightly weird. She's from Milena too, he told himself, how did I manage not to see her, I must have
gone to school with her as a kid, how come I nearly
missed her? My father didn't understand what had
suddenly opened his eyes, whether he had just
emerged from a deep sleep or whether she had
undergone a metamorphosis.

He went on posting himself in the same place
every day, illicitly selling his made-to-measure
smokes and watching out for her, regularly running
an anxious hand over his head, which was close-
shaven just as it had to be.

At the time he even thought to himself, this is a
girl I could take with me when I go on the run. He
thought this because of the imagery of wide open
spaces, Thunderbirds, saturated guitar chords, and
gas stations waiting to be robbed out in the desert.

Not talking to her directly, with a bit of persist-
ence, seemed like the best way of establishing a connection with this creature.

He did try to find out about her, affecting all the
offhand disinterest of a detective, but also experiencing the disturbing satisfaction of talking about
her as often as possible, even to virtual strangers in
the high school—and talking about her filled him
with gratitude. He didn't reap anything particularly
convincing from it: he was told she was a lesbian,
but in those days that was a reputation often given

to pretty girls who were a bit distant.

My father was fifteen years old.

If Rose had looked at him as she went past the covered yard, she might have noticed his intensity, the intensity of his being there, she might have thought, I like that guy with his bad-boy look. But Rose didn't notice or think about anyone. She was just a princess, with her tall headdress and her veils, her eight-meter train and her bracelets jingling on her wrists.

FOUR

THAT SUMMER MOMMY ROSE AND I spent a lot of time on the roof of the building where we lived with Mr. Loyal in the Rue du Roi-Charles. We lived in the north of Camerone on a hillside, the side of one of the five hills of Camerone. The town was like lava, flowing down the slopes and forming a glutinous mass on the shore. The buildings in the upper town were white, dilapidated, and perched with dizzying views, proof of the recreational activities enjoyed there in better times. For a long time Camerone had been a seaside resort whose mild flower-filled winters attracted beautiful women and their wealthy gentlemen. Then this well-off population gradually depleted—probably preferring more exotic skies than these—and the masses came to invade the coast for the long stifling Camerone summers.

I liked living in Camerone because you could smell the sea and the cheap coconut oil, because its fall from grace lent it a sort of decadent languor—

the old women of Camerone still carried *broderie anglaise* parasols along the seafront promenade and were offended by the giggling groups of girls in their skimpy cotton sarongs. What I particularly liked was the sun's searing attack throughout the impressive succession of blue summer days. I watched Camerone steam from right up on the roof of our building on the Rue du Roi-Charles, on that wide terrace pounded by the heat—heat not unlike a molten metal or a glassblower's kiln, altering the elements and distorting them to suit itself. I stayed close to the hutches because I savored their smell and the constant rustle of tiny lives. I hobbled over the disjointed gravel-set-in-concrete paving stones of the terrace and scratched at the moss in the joints with my index finger—fascinating how determined vegetation can be to colonize territory perched so high up— blackening my nail and inspecting it closely in the hopes of detecting a minute reptilian world. I was usually stripped to the waist with faded panties and a black cape tied at the neck. My sweat created salty landscapes on the lining of my cape. I scrubbed them with soap and water in the evenings so that the wretched cape would stay spotless and operational.

I was fifteen years old. But my age didn't mean anything. I was a very old woman on the inside—an old woman full of wisdom, mom said—someone who could reason, who panicked at the thought of how many centimeters she had left to live, a woman with a very long memory and moments of terrible confusion. And seen from the outside, I was a fat little girl who had no plans to grow or to start her periods anytime soon, or to have to think seriously about going to high school more regularly—in a normal school, that is. (Mom would have added, you're not fat, you're not fat, you're not fat, you've got sex appeal to burn, trust me.)

I could see the horizon, a horizon of roof terraces, a bric-a-brac of TV antennas, satellite dishes, water tanks, clandestine gardens with bamboo and fences and receptacles to catch the acid rain, chairs, crates acting as footrests, refrigerators for beer, their generators whirring night and day; there were also the stray cats, the seagulls, the sirens, and the gasping sounds from the port. The noise from the streets wafted up to us in lazy snatches. I would always think, they could easily all die down there, they could all get the plague, and we wouldn't know anything about it, me and my rabbits.

The rabbits were huddled under the shade of the chimney stack, they had small fans to ensure they had a bit of air, so that they didn't pass out but carried on gazing at the roofs-and-terraces horizon in front of them.

We understood each other perfectly, my rabbits and me.

They wore such shimmering colors, some had long fluffy coats, so much so that you could be forgiven for thinking they were out of focus, others had dull eyes or were completely blind and reproduced in darkness. We were inundated with baby rabbits. So to counter the invasion—and therefore our own elimination—we ate them, and as a way of buying favor with the inhabitants of the building on the Rue du Roi-Charles, we would cut them up and give these skinned offerings to our recalcitrant neighbors. I liked eating my rabbits. It meant I could stay with them forever.

I spent most of my time on the terrace near the rabbits (that I would soon be eating), sitting on a small red wooden chair, concentrating on catching a dazzling patch of the ocean between two buildings. I willingly let my retina burn when it blinded me like that—the flash of light streaking toward my eye, brilliant and bewitching, my own treasure burning my eyes and eating away at my optic nerve.

Mom didn't stay on the terrace as long as me, she had things to see to. From time to time she would come up to say she was going out or to the shop, or to tell me my snack was ready. I saw her emerging from the trapdoor, she was very beautiful, carrying a pretty plastic purse that gleamed as if she had been rubbing it all night with a felt cloth. Sometimes she would ask, do you think I have a little bit far too much makeup on? and I would say no with a shake of my head, even though I felt my opinion couldn't matter less because I didn't know anything about women or women's attire, all I knew about was my terrace, the institute I was packed off to some evenings, and the trip I sometimes made on my own between the terrace and the aforementioned institute. I was grateful to her for asking me. I watched her leave and hoped I would be like her one day.

I often let my snack disintegrate and dribble over the tablecloth in the kitchen or sometimes I would go and fetch it and get myself all sticky on the way back up to the terrace.

How the summer vacation dragged on.

I didn't have to think about the Institute I would soon be going back to, my special school, as they called it, my parents. I used to hear them talking about it to Mrs. Isis or another neighbor, they would say, our little girl goes to a special school for exceptionally talented children or a school for raving lunatics. People never asked any questions, they smiled and nodded their heads as if they understood, but their eyes betrayed a particular kind of panic, terrified because neither my father nor my mother would elaborate on the subject. I watched them do it and wondered whether my parents were ashamed or simply tired of explaining and preferred

VÉRONIQUE OVALDÉ

just to sigh and hope people would reach their own conclusions.

When dusk came I would lean over from the rooftop and watch people's heads as they passed by down below. The blue evening shadows looked damp from up there, the road was so deep down and so far from the intense clarity of my terrace, I could make out the pitching and hissing of cars, and I tried to spot mom's wig. I waited up there in studied immobility—if I move, everything falls apart—watching out for her—if I move, she won't come back.

From the open windows of our building I could hear the sputtering chitchat of radios or mellow bossa nova coming straight from Mrs. Isis's apartment. And then I would see mom coming around the end of the street, she still had her shiny polished plastic purse and shopping bags full of milk, breakfast cereals, vegetables that an old woman she knew gave to her, and perhaps some meat for my father the circus manager. Yes, it was definitely her all the way down there with that gleaming hair. She was walking quickly, not moving her doll-like blond head too much, I could almost hear the click-clack of her heels. I waited until she went into the building, the heels on her shoes were unbelievable, she disappeared under the porch, they were dangerously high, I think the man who designed them must have said, if any woman manages to wear

18

them, I'll marry her, she'll have the perfect feet for my perfect shoes.

I hurried down from the terrace to meet her, bursting onto the landing before she got there, waiting for the elevator to clang and let me know she had arrived safely. She pushed the door open with her shoulder: she was gorgeous. And that was when I always wondered—just as she appeared before me with her blond wig, the heels I found so terrifying, and the dark rings under her eyes—I always wondered why she had had a daughter like me, given that she was so gorgeous.

FIVE

MY NAME IS ROSE LIKE MY MOTHER.

Not Rose b, not Rose II, or Rosebud, Rosalie, Rosette, Rosa Niña, Seven Sisters Rose, or Rosa Gallica. No, I'm just called Rose, like her.

I think it was my father who decided to call me that. My father the circus manager. I don't want to know, I've never wanted to know, I'm only guessing why I have the same name as my mother.

And every time I think about it I feel myself sinking into a long, deep, cool well, and the bottom of the well is way down at the end, slippery with moss and damp rock, the chill humidity penetrating my lungs and the bones of my ankles. I rest my ass on the red mushrooms, which crumble and give off a smell like seashells.

I stay in that shady place with a big circle of sky up above, breathing cautiously and repeating the words: my name is Rose like my mother.

—

I knew that my mother came from somewhere much farther north than Camerone. She told me about it and she even mentioned it to her friends sometimes—the ones who came in the evening when Mr. Loyal wasn't there. With me her voice would be very soft and slow, as if she were telling a fairy tale with a forest, a clearing, and in the middle of the clearing, a marshmallow cottage dusted with powdered sugar. With her friends she danced around the subject and made jokes about the heat in Camerone, the "tropics," she always said. She conjured up the lakes and the fir trees and the snow, shaking her head and wrinkling her nose when she described the neat rows of palm trees along the seafront in our town.

She said, where I come from there was a gold mine.

She said, the little town we lived in was hemmed in by the mountains and was called Milena. A river ran through it, a river that started out as a torrent tumbling down from the pass, then settled as it ran beneath the stone bridges of Milena and picked up its hectic pace again farther down.

She said, all the men worked at the gold mine. My father worked at the gold mine and my two brothers did too when they were old enough to leave school. At first there were mines in the mountains, along the river, with water cannons and big mechanical contraptions that delved into the bottom of the river to dig away at the ancient riverbed. Later, when all the gold had gone from the mountains, the men came down into the valley, they drilled boreholes and found that there was still lots of gold to be had there, so they settled there, any old way at first, with makeshift houses, before they eventually brought their wives there. A village grew up, with a church, a local council, and schools, and soon it was a town with a stadium, a station, and regular trains bringing in guys hungry for gold. They dug basins, which they filled with a cyanide solution, they extracted the ore and left it in these blue pools, they dried the metal in kilns, shaped and weighed cylinders of rough gold, took them to the smelting works two hundred kilometers away, and made 9,999 grade ingots—99.99 percent pure. They knew that one day the gold might run out, they would say, metal is crafty, and there's none wilier than gold. They lived in that valley, peering into the cyanide pools, with their big boots, their gloves, their raincoats, and they saw birds fall out of the sky when they flew over the pools, but that didn't bother them, they would just shake their heads and say, it might all be over soon, let's make the most of it, don't let's forget that gold's a sly metal.

Mom told me about it a little at a time. Her memories of the gold mine fired everyone's imagination. Some of her friends asked her where Milena was and she would say, there isn't any gold left now, no point going there, it's all over, the gold's gone. The fact that they thought her past was like something out of a book made her laugh. They would sip their drinks and watch her, thinking, I'm sure they were thinking, we're so lucky she came down from her mountains, we're so lucky she came here, to us.

Mommy Rose sometimes shook her fake hair, and one of them, slumped in Mr. Loyal's armchair, drinking Mr. Loyal's gin, stroking the arm of Mr. Loyal's wife, would say, take off your wig, sweetheart, you're going to boil under there, because he couldn't possiby imagine what was under that wig: he thought it was vanity, the insensitive creep, he thought her real hair was lank and red and that she preferred this lush blond hair, he could only see it as artifice, the misplaced idiot. Obviously she refused to take off her wig, she did it very gently, mind you, shaking her head and smiling, apparently not even resenting the creep for his request, forgiving his curiosity with the wing-beat of her eyelashes, which meant, I'm so far removed from you all, I do what I can, my friends, but I'm so far from you. Mommy Rose refused because she couldn't show them her scalp, she couldn't show them the left hemisphere with its Martian surface, the burned epidermis, and the tender color of it like the inside of a mouth.

—

With me she revealed her tortured scalp.

In the mornings when my father, Mr. Loyal, was away, she walked about the apartment in a flesh-colored lacy nylon slip. I would pass really close to her so that I could scrunch the fabric with my nails.

There was something noble and decrepit about the apartment on the Rue du Roi-Charles, which made it feel like an ancient fountain. It centered around the living room (the walls crazed with cracks obeying some urgent, secret rhythm, plaster and polystyrene moldings like dusty designs in meringue) and there was a little kitchen with a polished stone floor, smooth as a millstone, and walls you could have dug mushroom beds in, so damp they seemed ideal for cryptogramic life. There was my pantry bedroom, my hidden bedroom behind a door with a mirror on it like a wardrobe, requiring the subtlest pressure with the fingertips to operate the mechanism, the door in question opening slowly, a clandestine place, a wartime hideout; inside, in the shadows, my bed, just enough room for my bed, a stool with clothes piled onto it, and my radio, small and gray with its overdeveloped aerial reaching toward the wire netting of the window.

In the apartment on the Rue du Roi-Charles there was also Mr. Loyal and my mother's bedroom, brimming with satin and rococo details, the unmade bed—and, of course, that state of abandon smacked of luxury—muslin curtains always drawn, but as the room faced due south it was often bathed in rosy light. My mother would only raise the drapes in order to lean against the railings above the street and the palm trees, assiduously trimming her nails with a gleaming little tool, letting the tiny clippings fall onto the passersby way below, humming a tune punctuated by the regular clicking sound of the hinged instrument. Click-clack mommy humming up above the street, gazing down on the beetles beneath her.

The last room in the apartment was the bathroom, invaded by bottles of perfume and creams promising eternal youth, a bathtub for near midgets, a slipper-bath, she called it, a *slipper*-bath, and I wondered, do they make ankle-boot-baths, stiletto-heel-baths, thigh-high-boot ones, do they make baths that would fit my father?

In the mornings my mother dragged her feet on the floor tiles, wandering around the apartment with her cup of tea, she already had her makeup on, coal-black eyes and glaring mouth, but it was so hot she couldn't sit down, her slip would have stuck to her buttocks, so she stayed standing, lighting her cigarette from the glowing butt of the previous one, reading a dog-eared paperback, a marshmallow romance, or leaning against the counter in the kitchen leafing through a magazine, or shaking the remote control from the far side of the counter to catch the infrared beam and change the TV station, an imperious gesture that fascinated me and that I imitated in front of the bathroom mirror. There she was, drifting up and down behind the closed shutters without her wig on, and I had all the time in the world—as I sat on the sofa, not giving a damn that the leatherette was sticking to my thighs and engraving little circuits on my skin—I had all the time in the world to study her head and the skin over it. She knew I was watching her, she played along with it, pretending she didn't care, oh, you're there, are you? knowing I would never dare ask a single question.

Did I when I was little? Did I put my baby hand on her head and ask her, what's this? her replying gently, it's my burned skin, and me insisting because I didn't understand, burned, how? and her thinking for a moment to find the most appropriate reply, making up her mind and stopping at that, saying, in a fire, but never making it clear what fire it was, as if she had chosen this option on a whim.

I ended up believing her scalp had ignited spontaneously. There she was, dancing in her new red dress, and suddenly half her head set on fire, everyone screamed and scattered as far from her as they could in the nightclub, and she fell to the floor, rolling and still burning.

I was allowed to see her tortured scalp but my father, Mr. Loyal, never saw it. I think he was the one who didn't want to. He would have turned away if she had taken off her wig like he turned away in the bathroom so he didn't have to watch her pee. Or maybe it was because her wounded skin conjured up expanses of my mother's past that could not possibly be conjured on the Rue du Roi-Charles.

It was something we kept between us, a girl thing (how to lose weight by eating cucumber, how to seduce a man just by gracefully swinging one foot, how to whisk eggs even when you have your period), it was a soothing motherly thing (now you know me better than anyone else), and I would say to myself, I don't know anything about her hair, all I know is the glossy artificial color of her Barbie wig, and her black eyebrows drawn on with eye pencil, in a thick symmetrical curve. There she is in her rayon slip with her perfect painted eyebrows, there she is, I look at her, absorb her, want to devour her, I want to know everything about her, I want to know what the infinite grace of her posture hinges on or the harmony of her face. I keep telling myself, I'm going to draw her, and I create imaginary grids to explain and preserve the perfection of her features. I must have a mathematical explanation for her beauty.

—

Then she would put her wig on, adjusting it with a myriad of little gestures and delicate details—curls behind the ears, kiss curls and ringlets straying out of the false bun, artificial abandon, deliberate mess. And she would leave for work.

My mother sold candy and ice cream on the seafront, in a sickly-smelling little store shoehorned between two palm trees, and those trees were planted by palm tree planers, with a carefully designed curve to give the impression they were stretching toward the sea, reaching for the light and the salt, heads held high like the prow of a ship, with the ocean dead ahead, but before the ocean was the sandy beach, with sand in just the right color, carefully selected, like its grain and texture, a heavenly beach conceived by a beach architect, tested out on the ground by beach engineers, and each dune constructed by beach builders. Mom hated the place, she said, that beach is like my hair.

She sold her ice creams as if it were an exquisite form of torture. When she finally left the site of her torment she went off to her dance class in a pretentious old house with bumpy paving stones in its inner courtyard and the endless splash of water and a marshy, mossy smell (it smells like a tomb, mom would say with a smile, and I thought she was being funny because when I looked at her in horror and she replied, it's okay, I'm joking, I'm joking, I'm

VÉRONIQUE OVALDÉ

joking). That was where the musicians were, the ones who came to the Rue du Roi-Charles in Mr. Loyal's absence, and young girls like birds, graceful in a feverish, feathery way. My mother was the oldest and the most vulgar—because of the contrast between her eyebrows and her hair—but the young doves would sigh languidly as they watched her, suspecting (as I did) that she harbored sexual mysteries, secrets to do with men's bodies.

Sometimes I was allowed to go with her, I wasn't always condemned to sweat it out on the terrace with my rabbits, smelling the sea air. I was allowed to go with her, and I would sit on the wooden floor in a corner of the room, near her bag and the piano. And mom would waft and pirouette past, leaving in her wake a smell of nougat and grilled pecans. In the background I could hear the doves swishing along the barres.

SIX

 One evening Mr. Loyal came home too early.

I was in bed in my tiny room with its minute wire-netted window (it didn't seem like a bedroom to me, but very much a pantry, a place where they would once have put hams and potatoes because it was cool, dark, and dry, and where I was now stowed away for the same reasons, it's the best place in the house, mommy used to say). I was asleep, and it was the sudden burst of loud voices from the living room that woke me. Mr. Loyal never normally shouted, apparently more at ease in an evanescent world than the real one, having chosen to adopt a rather poetic stance since his most sensitive childhood years and having exercised his peculiar profession—or rather, what I supposed his profession to be—without having too much to do with material things. I could picture him having a quick word with the acrobats before they went into the ring, asking anxiously about the old lion's toothache and

31

consoling the contortionist for her disappointments in love. I had never been under his big top for reasons related to my fragile emotional state and to the seedy part of town where the circus was situated. I had been promised a visit but I didn't insist. After all, it was just the place where Mr. Loyal worked, Mr. Loyal's office, his store. I had no idea what the words "circus manager" were hiding. As far as I was concerned, it was an acceptable profession, I had no reason to think there was cause for camouflage.

So I was woken by shouts and Mr. Loyal's bellowing voice. I could make out Mommy Rose's hurried explanations from her voluble excesses and the shrill tone she had adopted. I opened my eyes wide in the darkness to hear better, holding my breath and stiffening so that no incidental rustling dampened my acuity. A few of mom's friends were still there, she had prepared some nibbles for them—a word that reverberated like a rude joke—and had brought in provisions of gin. I had stayed with them for a while and then gone to bed because I felt gloomy and tearful, and mom would always say, *I think you're tired* three times the minute she heard me moan or caught me wilting like a tulip. We had agreed, she and I, that I could stay at these evening gatherings only if I could recognize the onset of my exhaustion myself.

I listened with all the concentration of a concert

pianist, they're only friends, I heard her squeal, and I could hear the subterranean rumblings of my father's voice but couldn't make out what he was saying, and her going on in the same tone of voice: you really ought to trust me, and him: but where are they from? and her: they're musicians from my dance class, and him, not wanting to stop in full flow, ready to do battle now, starting to talk about depravity and a dissolute life, her interrupting him, speaking over him, not very loudly but on a different frequency to Mr. Loyal, almost whispering, but in a stubborn, very deliberate whisper that was worse than a scream, a hiss of steam, her holding her ground: they're friends, we're just hanging out together, Loulou (who was she talking to? to Mr. Loyal? Loulou? she never called him anything but Mr. Loyal in front of me, was this—this Loulou—a name connected to their intimate relationship? was it possible that she went on calling him Mr. Loyal when she was naked with him in their bed, or had she chosen to opt for something more tender and ridiculous like Loulou?). I heard a voice that was distinct from theirs making a point: I've got my guitar, you can see that, and Mr. Loyal roaring again quite loudly: do these wasters come here often? then his onslaught stopping dead and, because he was now slamming doors, her saying, please, the little one's asleep, and him carrying on mumbling and saying things like, give me some goddamn peace, and, this is my house, and lots of other things I couldn't make out, I heard cupboards and the refrigerator being opened and closed, and him still going on, this is my house, go and have your fucking parties somewhere else, still slamming doors, turning faucets as if to check the water pressure, while I huddled in my pantry, exhausted by the intensity of my own curiosity and my concentration, rapt with fear, and if they separate, who would I stay with? and mom cutting everything dead, seeing her friends out, going down to the main entrance with them, him carrying on growling to himself in the kitchen, fuck off out of here, go and drink some other sap's liquor somewhere else, while Mommy Rose went down the stairs with her friends, hugging her little yellow openwork cardigan over her chest, waving to them as they walked away, and going back up slowly, deciding she would be in a bad mood with my father so that he couldn't be in one with her, not uttering one word to him, and curling up in a ball in her armchair to sleep in the living room rather than with him in the bedroom, the wig probably very slightly askew, given her position, not deigning to speak to him again for a tidy ten days, indignant as she was, standing on her virtue, and him quickly getting over his temper, no longer grousing, and trying to speak to her the very next morning, casting flies and bait and downright silver spoons, trying to ask questions about me that she couldn't just answer with a nod of the head, calling her princess when she looked down on him haughtily…all the same, my father didn't want to apologize but was keen, as he always was, to express his goodwill and his unshakeable devotion.

SEVEN

MOM TOLD ME ABOUT HER BROTHERS. It was a Thursday. The summer was coming to an end. I had already gone back to the Institute, but on a provisional basis, only in the morning, not in the afternoon, or at night of course. I remember clearly that it was a Thursday because I had a little calendar that I changed daily. It gave me intense satisfaction tearing off a page every morning, amazed that each day passed and none of them had the same name, that this could happen seven times in a row and then the phenomenon began again indefinitely like some divine mechanism.

I'm the third in the family, she told me.

She had come up to see me on the roof that evening, poking her fingers through the bars of the hutches, wiggling one finger to attract the rabbits' taciturn attention. They glanced up, carried on crinkling their pink noses, interrupting their obsessive masticating for a moment—and I wondered, if they stop will their teeth start growing until they cut through their gums and come out the other side?

I was the third, mom said again.

There was Charles and there was Franck.

Dusk was falling and the sun was disappearing behind the sea. Her nylon hair gleamed.

Charles was the oldest. He was more gentle.

Franck came second. He was terrible, he would never let me go out alone. Franck was so jealous it was crazy.

She sat down next to me on one of the two tiny chairs on the terrace, by my toy tea set, so pretty but broken and stuck back together and with one orphaned teacup, like a real tea service struck down by a curse: *you shall shrink and turn into a doll's tea set*. I had an indefinable light-headed sensation when I used that tiny tea set, it filled me with despair, as if confronting my own inability to fit into the world, and I reveled in the heartbreak of it.

She's talking to me about her brothers, I thought, probably so that she can get around to talking about my father. It starts with Franck and Charles and goes on to my father.

I served her a make-believe cup of tea with my make-believe tea set. She pretended to drink it and enjoy it, sighing in the sinking sunlight and telling me rather inappropriately, you're quite the cordon-bleu, which made me think of an exotic bird, a hummingbird with electric-colored plumage.

Oh, if Franck hadn't kept me indoors all the time, we wouldn't have come to this.

I mulled over this pronouncement with her, abstaining from any questions, not daring to penetrate the mysteries of Mommy Rose and her unfathomable regrets, suspecting that I was also at the nerve center of her melancholy, if Franck hadn't kept her indoors all the time, I wouldn't be there or maybe not in this state, nodding slowly as I held the make-believe teapot with my little finger raised to give mom the impression I was much more refined than people might think. She looked at me, put her arm around my shoulder, and kissed my neck. I could hear her sniffing the nape of my neck and my hair, and sighing with satisfaction because my bodily odors, the smell of any of my secretions never disgusted her; she seemed instead to find them utterly delicious.

Franck and Charles worked at the gold mine, she went on. They made it a point of honor to be as punctual, honest, and sensible as possible. We lived with our mother in a house up above the forest, on the mountainside with part of the house dug into the rock and there, in the washhouse where my brothers kept their liquor, the temperature was always the same however deep the snow outside or however hot the July sun, as if the center of things was stable and it never let that permanence be disturbed by the vagaries of the outside world.

I let my mother purr gently, so she went on.

When my father took a hike, Charles was fifteen, Franck was twelve, and I was four. My mother showed such courage and determination that she managed to end up without all of Milena pitted against her despite the circumstances and the old man's disappearance. He was responsible for the security of a cargo of gold when it was loaded into the helicopter heading for the foundry (and I thought to myself, shit, here she is talking about her father and I want her to talk about mine), he and a friend held everyone up and gunned down one of the guys with them, then he made off with his henchman, who could fly the contraption—they found the guy with a bullet between the eyes a few days later, three hundred kilometers away. I was only four at the time, can you imagine? I never saw my father again, he never came back. So, my little Rose, don't go thinking, just don't go thinking he could still come back now with rings on all his fingers, wanting to make up for his crimes and set us up like a couple of countesses. I longed for that my whole childhood. But he never came back. You have to face the facts. He was an asshole.

Why's she telling me all this, I wondered, why doesn't she tell me about my father instead, the real

real one?

But she didn't say anything about him that evening, she went on with her stories about gold mines and valiant brothers, she carried on talking about her mother, who went to the high school every other evening to sing stuff about God and his saints to make sure Milena didn't turn its back on her once and for all, to keep a little place for herself in their little town. I ran my hand over my eyes, I've got a headache, I thought, and then corrected myself: where exactly does my head ache? and I stopped listening to what she was saying about brothers number one and number two, I had decided not to listen to anything so long as she wasn't talking about my father, I let her carry on while I thought, my throat's sore too because of all these questions about my father stuck in my gullet, questions I'll never dare ask, I didn't take an interest in what she was saying, it seemed to me she was tracing an ellipse around a mother star that she didn't want to touch on. I silently told her, go on, talk, talk, that's right, keep talking and carefully avoiding the subject, I granted myself the right to be irreverent in silence. But what is she doing? I asked myself, it's like she's diving into a lake, like she doesn't want to or can't come up to the surface for more than a moment, like she's taking a lungful of air and going back under, and her breaths are spaced farther and farther apart. What is she looking for? I asked myself. I sighed discreetly and hummed to myself so that I didn't have to listen to her.

—

And the very next morning, that Friday morning, Mommy Rose started waiting for the newspaper and reading it with a suspicious degree of attention.

I could tell that these events had a specific timely cause, I suspected this was not just the conjunction of a few minor incidents; I couldn't imagine this sequence of things stemming from anything other than a thunderbolt. So I told myself something must have happened, something that made her tell me about her brothers and stand watch by the window, lying in wait behind the shutters so that she could get the first glimpse of the paperboy as he came around the end of the street.

It was the first morning she did that.

And she didn't let up on that ritual until the end.

She was looking for something.

She would sit at the kitchen table and spread the pages carefully over the Formica, smoothing the paper and scouring over the columns of text, forgetting her cigarette hanging in the right-hand corner of her mouth, closing the corresponding eyelid with a slight grimace—a fatal, seductive grimace—and I would sit facing her with a cushion under my buttocks, registering her every move so that I could reproduce them in apposite moments. She spent ages picking through each tiny new item, she's looking for something that's not printed, I told myself, something written in friendly ink, something invisible to the naked eye, are there lines between the lines, letters between the letters, is there a woodcutter hidden in this forest of letters? and one day I asked her, I said, did you find the woodcutter? but she didn't look up, she just said, I don't know what you mean, and she carried on scanning the personal ads.

That Friday morning, the first Friday of Mommy Rose's obsession, Mr. Loyal took me to the beach. I think he wanted to get away from the house for a few hours, that he knew something wasn't quite right, that he had to get himself out of there, and that it would be easier and more enjoyable with me. We took the bus, him and me, the one that went really fast with all the windows open, making a deafening noise—my hair blew in every direction, it felt like it was suddenly going to be torn out by the whirling wind—and he took me to the beach.

Mr. Loyal had a big stomach, a big ass, and breasts almost like a woman. He sweated profusely, I liked his sweat and his skin, which was always soft and wet—like the piece of cloth mom used to iron his shirts, it was soaked with water but didn't drip on the floor, and it transformed into a cloud of steam.

Mr. Loyal wore suspenders.

I always thought: his shoulders are holding his pants up, and it fascinated me, that solidarity between different organs—the deficient waist supported by the fat carcass.

We went to Swordfish Beach, look at the sky, he said, look at the sky, Rose, he took my hand, he was wearing white pants, the suspenders against the bare skin of his stomach, an open shirt, and a wide, stained hat, he took my hand and we walked down to that small steep-sided beach where the sea glittered like treasure.

We undressed, me dropping my clothes onto the sand, him folding his conscientiously, the label of his trunks hanging out at the back. It was amazing how that label was never on the inside. I don't know why but I never told him he should cut it off or push it in, I found that label touching and reassuring, and I always made sure I was behind my father so I could keep my eyes on that label—which was actually nothing more than a scrap of frayed, faded white fabric now. And I would tell myself, I recognize my father by that hanging label, the day that he takes off his pants and the label on his trunks is no longer visible, I'll know someone else has taken his place, I'll know that that extraterrestrial isn't my father.

We went for a swim and he became graceful, feather-light, we played in the water, it was still very early, there were just one or two surfers lying on their boards waiting, breathing the salty morning air, and I thought, they're so patient! and I suspected that they weren't really hoping for a wave, these boys: they came at dawn and pointed their faces into the breeze, watching the languid waves and paddling gently, lost in thought.

Then the circus manager and I dried off in the sun, listening to the surf and the tiny sound of the sand constantly modifying its dunes in an imperceptible millennial motion. I tried desperately to make out the sound of the sand moving.

Then we ran to catch the bus—me skipping along and the circus manager making the surface of the globe shudder. He dropped me at the Institute with a sick note, no one commented on my dripping hair or the smell of salt or the sand in the folds of my neck or my wet sandals, no one believed his sick note, everyone smiled and my father went home to take shelter behind the shutters.

That's all I remember from that time, mom waiting anxiously for the paperboy to arrive, and the sound of the sand making dunes.

EIGHT

THE NEWSPAPER ARRIVED.

It was morning, my father the circus manager had just come out of the bathroom, he spent a lot of time in that tiny room with its blue enamelware—did he have some technique for dancing twirls in there, going from the mirror to the cupboard, from the child-size slipper-bath to the basin, how does he manage to turn around when he's inside that place, I wondered. He spent a lot of time looking after his teeth (ravaged by his excessive sugar consumption) and his skin, trying to make it smoother, softer, and more tender than the sole of a baby's foot, almost peeling his cheeks raw with his polishing.

I was there, with them, every morning. It was a phase when I was trying to behave as well as possible, when I was so gentle and charming that I heard them asking each other, wouldn't we do better to take her out of the Institute? or maybe I didn't hear them say that, I just hoped they would say it, perhaps they were wary of these periods of calm, or did they know me well enough to know that I could keep the mad girl slumbering at bay for a certain length of time, that I could leave her writhing without going near her, like a quicksilver fish in the bottom of a creel, that I could avoid touching her even with the tips of my fingers for weeks on end but then, inevitably, I would put my hand in and get an electric shock that would plunge me straight back into the storm. At the moment I was sitting on the edge of the creel, behaving as if I were about to take communion, so that I would be allowed to come home to sleep every evening, so they wouldn't make me spend the night at the Institute, with its savage unsociability, with the shadows and the hurtling doctors, the screams and the smell of food that gathered under my bed, that goddamn smell of food, boiled food, what the hell do they eat the whole time, it smells like grated carrots and boiled celery, there's never any pecan ice cream, there's never any sort of ice cream, just the occasional rancid sponge cake, something with fruits of the forest, powdery fruit that disintegrates into dust between your tongue and the roof of your mouth, I don't want to sleep at the Institute, the night people don't smile at me as much as the day people, they don't look after me, they look after the ones who scream and shit in their beds, the ones who have noisy thrashing nightmares, but I don't make any noise, I know how to be terrified in silence, I lie there prostrate, not moving a muscle, hardly breathing, trying to lose consciousness by my own means, the ones on the edge, concentrating and curling up so tight that there's no room left in my body for anything, cram me in and close the stopper, screw it down hard, I won't come undone again. No, I couldn't spend my nights at the Institute, I had to watch mom.

And that morning, like every morning, she had made his coffee for him.

It's ready, she shouted three times.

And, after ten minutes, your coffee's ready. It's cold.

She didn't cope well with his slow ablutions.

When he eventually left, when he put on his hat and winked at me as I got ready to go the Institute—gesticulating on the floor in my efforts to put on my sandals—when he opened the door, he let the paper delivery boy in.

That's not right, I thought.

He didn't normally meet the delivery boy. Today wasn't going to be like every other day.

I saw a sign.

I crossed my fingers on both hands, crossed my legs, my feet, the sandals, everything I could cross by way of exorcism. I hoped that my anxiety was more the conspiring sort than a premonition.

Mom very slowly took the newspaper from the delivery boy's hand, her nylon hair didn't move, it was like dead sugar shining on a creamy dessert, she very slowly closed the door and unfolded the news-paper, and she started to go out, like a lightbulb she started to go out.

It was because of that newspaper that she started to go out.

She laid it flat on the table and scoured through it minutely, turning the pages, methodically elimi-nating anything that didn't mention what she was hoping for. I couldn't wait any longer, I was going to be late. I said, I'm going to be late, mom. She stopped what she was doing halfway through turning a crackling page, yes, she said, do you want to go on your own, baby? I didn't want to go on my own. It was only in very special circumstances that I was allowed to go around the block to the Institute on my own, because I had performed some act of charity, because I had been beautifully behaved, because I had eaten and digested my broccoli without being sick all over the place from up on the terrace down onto Mrs. Isis's awning, at times like that my mother would say to my father, I think she can go there on her own, don't you think? and my father would look all important and nod his head in his infinite goodness, and say, yes, I think so too,

Rose, I think she can go on her own. On that particular day, I clenched my teeth and wondered
whether—on top of everything else that was
crossed—I was going to succeed in crossing my jaw,
can you say that, crossing your jaw? I had put my
sandals on the wrong feet, right on left and vice
versa, again as a way of warding off bad luck.

I walked out on the absolute tips of my toes,
closed the door very gently, and didn't go to the
Institute. I stayed at the foot of the building in the
square opposite the Rue du Roi-Charles, scanning
the pavement. And with the money for my lunch—
to buy breaded fish, peas, a yogurt, and rancid cake,
to hand over the money at the cash register at the
Institute in exchange for an orange polyurethane
food tray in the cafeteria with its smell of stale old
grease—I went to the joke shop nearby, right there,
on the right-hand side of the square, still in sight,
not taking my eyes off the building, bumping into
people in the street, but not taking my eyes off the
building, choosing a new cape with a pink satin
lining without really looking at it, still not taking my
eyes off the building, not listening to a word the
shopkeeper was saying, preoccupied with that door,
the door to the building, which I mustn't take my
eyes off, convinced that it would imprint itself, that
door would, on my retina, and that if mom came
out, I might not even see her, because the ghost of

that door would persist on my crystalline lens.

I went back to the square—with its palm trees, its rose garden, my lookout post—creeping sideways like a crab.

I waited all day, hiding under the oleanders.

Dusk fell.

She hadn't come out, unless she had found some other way to disappear, my head was spinning, I was sitting on the bare earth, which was so dry it was killing my coccyx. It's time to go back up, I told myself.

The constant noise of traffic outside the building, the yellow cloud of pollution rising up from the cars, battered against my head, insistent as a stormy sea. I held on to the tree to stand up, gazing at the white roses, which looked phosphorescent in the gathering gloom. I stayed there a moment to let myself come back to life in that phosphorescence. I folded my cape up into my backpack and crossed the street to go home.

—

Like a lightbulb, she had gone out.

She had not moved since morning, she was just sitting in front of that newspaper not moving a hair.

I found it incredibly hard to breathe, suffocating there with my backpack, my wrong-way-around sandals, and my cape folded up really tight— shining in the darkness of my backpack with all the brilliance of something magical and indestructible.

Didn't you go to the store, I asked, my voice all rusty from the carbon dioxide in the air on the square. She shook her head.

She didn't say anything, she didn't mention whether the Institute had rung to see why I wasn't there, I grasped that she hadn't been in a fit state to answer the phone anyway.

I opened the refrigerator and took some milk and a caramel-flavored dessert—a gelatinous thing that wobbled gently when I prodded it with my spoon, it moved the way I imagined breast flesh would move.

I sat down at the table facing her and put down my quivering dessert, making as little noise as possible with my spoon and my swallowing but getting the feeling that, in spite of my efforts, I was creating an unbearable racket with my snack, clanking my spoon against the china and freezing my hand with a grimace, then carrying on with slothlike slowness.

Mom still sat there inert.

I thought she was posing, *she's posing*, I told myself, for someone I can't see but who is in the room, someone who wants her to stay completely still.

Are you sad because of daddy? I said.

She stared at me as if I had uttered something shameful.

Because he gets home too late, because he's not here and you have too much to do? (I was throwing out buoys, trying to play her game, to pick up on her usual complaints, but I was just tying myself in knots).

In the end she gave a very small smile. She shook her head, folded her newspaper, took off her wig, and stood up, heading toward the bedroom, still holding her hair as if some long-haired animal had latched onto her hand.

I sighed.

I went to get myself some ice cream from the refrigerator. And I waited for Mr. Loyal to come home.

NINE

MR. LOYAL DIDN'T KNOW WHAT TO DO.

His arms hung limply by his side and he said, she's just a bit sad, a bit tired, she needs to be left alone.

But after a week I realized that she was gradually disappearing in front of the TV, well and truly disappearing, it already seemed as if she had almost been absorbed by the chenille armchair, I saw her a little less distinctly every day, her outline was becoming hazy.

Something's got to happen, I told myself.

I thought about it, but couldn't really think what to do.

Asking her about it would have been impossible. She had built a transparent plastic bubble around herself, with an anti-knock, anti-pollution, anti-question surface in a smooth, squdgy, impenetrable texture.

So I decided to throw myself out of the window.

I wasn't afraid of anything, I had my new cape with the fuchsia satin lining. I can see now that my reaction wasn't rational but obviously I didn't analyze all the implications of what I was doing.

I did the thing with an almost casual air, a sort of laughing complacency, in the same way that I might have hopped onto the last car of a train passing through the Russian mountains. Thinking about it too much would have diminished the capacity for jubilation in what I was doing. I went at it with panache.

I tumbled down, tearing Mrs. Isis's awning three floors farther down, taking the whole contraption along with me, and landing on a cornice, bound tightly inside the fabric of the awning like a parachutist strung up in a tree.

Mrs. Isis's awning saved me.

I decided it was thanks to my cape with the fuchsia satin lining.

I heard mom howling—and her howling was like a siren warning that there was a fire, or the imminent approach of a squadron of bombers, or a toxic cloud, it was a howl of warning not a howl of horrified surprise, she was just at her window letting the whole neighborhood know what her daughter had done, her little daughter who was still such a long way from the uncertainties of adolescence, yes, her Rose, who was still so little she shouldn't have been drawn into the abyss yet, that comes later, she must have said to herself over and over, I don't understand, that should have come much later.

—

When I fell I had the most intense feeling of relief, something not unlike euphoria, a euphoria very slightly tainted with despondency, like a rather exhausting sense of fulfillment. I don't know how to describe more precisely the feeling that pervaded my body and penetrated my blood and its enucleated elements, I felt a sort of limp well-being.

Then I got wound up in kind Mrs. Isis's awning with its yellow and white stripes splattered with every kind of shit. I took her canary cage with me as I fell. The bird opened its wings but couldn't do a thing, imprisoned as it was, suspended within the falling cage.

So there was a pale yellow, feathered victim. I came away distraught about it and I cried and cried over his tiny broken bones as I lay in my hospital bed.

TEN

AND THEY KEPT SAYING, WHY DID YOU JUMP? and I
knew what I had to tell them, I knew the answer but
I looked at them all innocently. If I'd known that
mom—right when the psychologists in the hospital
were asking, why did you jump?—if I'd known that
she had taken her clicks and her clacks (not even
them, in fact, she hadn't taken anything, not clicks
or clacks, just her black sandals and her black shirtdress with tiny, tiny sequins on it making a sort of
constellation), if I'd known she was getting out, and
the way she had chosen to do it, dissolving into
space, black sandals, black shirtdress with the glittering Milky Way on it, if I'd known, I would have
jumped out of my chair, I would have run through
the streets, I would have run as fast as a comet, just
like in my dreams, and I would have stopped her
from disappearing.

But all they could do was keep saying, why did
you jump? and I told them I hadn't wanted to jump,

I just wanted to try out my cape with the fuchsia lining—imagine that fierce geranium color, palpitating and brilliant like foliage in July sunlight. They couldn't understand—or they suspected I was playing some dirty trick on them—so they just went on asking the same question: they were probably less stupid than I thought, they had sniffed out a hoax. They said, we won't tell anyone, you can trust us completely—but I didn't trust anyone, except for my rabbits, I didn't trust mom, who, I knew, had to be watched, I didn't trust daddy because he wasn't the real one, the one who squirted, and in spite of everything, that made a difference. So you see, I could never have trusted the hospital psychologists. I smiled at them. Trust us, they kept saying, and I acted all amazed, how could I not trust you guys with your pretty white coats, which don't even have any bloodstains on them, your eyes are so clear and so honest, your hands shake only slightly—abusing the drugs store?—but that's a reassuring thing, those hands with their slight shaking, it makes you accessible, so you're not actually perfect androids, are your parents kind to you? I looked at them and I pictured their wives, their children, their mistresses, their houses, and their Range Rovers, and school, how's school going? they were still trying to get an answer, something that would bolster the diagnoses already written up in the files before I even opened my mouth, they would take pride in folding me up small and pressing down on my head so I fit into the box, so I didn't waver from the file hanging in the filing cabinet, so I didn't destroy their dogma with my incongruous answers, no no no, everything's fine, I just wanted to test the resistance of the fabric and the resistance of my body to the shock-crash-squishing-pulverizing.

They left me sitting on my low chair, I looked at my foot, which was bare because I had taken off my shoe, and ran my big toe up the corner of the chipped wooden desk—like a school desk, in fact, and that got me wondering whether it had dusty pink globs of chewing gum stuck underneath it. They consulted each other, I could hear them talking, I could hear them whispering in the room next door, their hushed voices crept under the door while my big toe went up and down, I knew what they were saying, they had asked me the right questions—is anyone ever unkind to you? and none of the children at the Institute give you a hard time?—that's what they kept asking, do the children give you a hard time? and debating about the validity of the Institute if the little patients went home to their parents only to throw themselves out the window, and while all this was going on, I tried out divination techniques: if I stare at the sun for three seconds, one two three, without blinking, I'll get out of here quickly, and—seeing I'm so good at hop-scotch—if I touch the joint between the squares on the linoleum, there will be a thunderstorm, and there they were talking about obsessive personalities, and still whispering, trying determinedly and methodically to identify who was hurting me, because that was what their questions always boiled down to, is your mother your father a child at the Institute, or even, oh damnation, an adult at the Institute ever unkind to you? You see they couldn't imagine that this was simply to do with me, me who might not wish me well, me against me, me all alone against me.

ELEVEN

MY FATHER, MR. LOYAL, took exemplary care of me
after my mother disappeared.

She's gone, he told me soberly when I got back
to the apartment after my time in the hospital,
where I had been so good that the psychologists had
had no choice but to prescribe me some pills, some
rest, and weekly counseling sessions. She's gone, he
said in the same way he might have said, I've forgotten to put the laundry away, or wouldn't you
rather have vanilla and macadamia nut?

When I wanted to know exactly when and why
and in what circumstances she had gone, he looked
at me, saddened by my curiosity, sighing at the
thought of the scenes he really had hoped I wouldn't
make, he just said, she didn't come home from the
store, I went there and back a dozen times, I went
and spoke to the shopkeepers she used to stop off
with on her way home, no one had seen her.

It was clear that she wasn't going to reappear,

that she hadn't just gone to the patisserie to get her favorite pastries, that she hadn't been kept late at her dance class, or that she hadn't had some problem with the metal shutter at the candy store (which happened quite regularly in the days when the world was still behaving the way it should), it was clear that eight days' absence was a long wait for a man alone in his apartment, a man who had to talk all sorts of twaddle—which was all swallowed quite placidly, mind you—to his little girl stuck in the hospital, keeping on saying, mommy's very busy at the store, she's a bit tired with all this going on, a man who wouldn't dare burden his little girl with any more worries while she was being kept in to recuperate, and justifiably suspecting the reservations the Institute and the hospital would have had about sending little Rose home to him if they had known her mother had disappeared.

The time will come, he must have kept thinking.

The time will come.

Time for me to fill my lungs with her absence when I came home, to be slapped full in the face by the dazed apathy in which the whole apartment was now suspended, to think, I just don't understand, this is the worst day of my life, to keep saying, this is the worst day and there have already been so many worst days, feeling my sternum retracting, my body drying out like a sponge on the terrace in full midday sun, my body becoming light, light and arid, hard and insubstantial.

How dare she leave without taking me with her?

I took mom's disappearance into my hands, rolled it up into a tight little ball, and swallowed it so the enemy wouldn't find it—they would have to slice me right down the middle—and I asked my father, I hope you looked after the rabbits, at least. Not putting as much reproach into that "at least" as he might have interpreted (you let *her* go, but I do hope you didn't abandon the rabbits, negligent though you are), simply using it to punctuate my sentence, so that it had a better rhythm to it. My father, Mr. Loyal, who was already sweating profusely, who was the sort of man who could drench his shirt, took me by the hand and took me up to the terrace to get some fresh air, to avoid any further evaporations, and to show me the good care he had taken of my rabbits. He kept saying, you see, my little cookie, I didn't forget them. And he was right, none of them had died of sunstroke, they were all well shaded, well tucked under the bamboo and the crates, which turned in time with the sun, thanks to a little motor he had set up himself. I said, thank you, thank you, and squeezed his wet hand even harder—the moisture on his palms embarrassed him, and to show that I didn't have a problem with it, I always kept my hand in his a little too long for comfort.

I think I'll stay up on the terrace with them for a bit, I said. He agreed, when any other parent would have thought, she's going to climb over the wall again.

He went back downstairs and I sat on my bench to mull over mom's absence at my leisure.

TWELVE

THE FIRST TWO DAYS AFTER I GOT BACK to the Rue du Roi-Charles I stayed at home, or to be more precise, on the terrace, sitting on my bench in the shade of the rabbit hutches.

I got up every fifteen minutes—a big brown alarm clock marked out the time for me—to check the street corner, right where she should eventually have appeared with her blond wig gleaming in the sun so that she single-handedly lit up the filthy sidewalk and the blaring street.

When I grew tired of getting up like a metronome, I set up the two mirrors from the bathroom in the corner of the terrace so that they would inform me of her potential return right where I was sitting.

The rest of the time I looked at photos.

After trying to lay my hands on the fatal newspaper and failing—although I had looked for it without really believing in my search, more or less

convinced that she had disappeared with her newspaper—I went up to the terrace with the whole
freight of albums and the motley collection of wal-
lets, transparent ones and cardboard ones, in which
mom, with her prehistoric sense of organization,
had stored dozens of sets of prints with no respect
to chronology or theme (holidays, the beach) or
affection (the trees I love, little Rose with her bucket).

Using my own occult systems, I sorted through
them, making little piles on the paving stones with
tufts of grass pushing up in the gaps, I put them in
order with the obscure conviction that the mystery
of her disappearance would vanish abruptly.

In the photos mom had hair. It looked red but
the snapshots had all tended toward a rusty rosy
color—unless the world really was rusty and rosy
when my mother was a child, and dresses all had
those sickly creamy dominant colors, and everyone's
complexion was slightly blotchy, and the sky was a
constant sandstorm.

I looked at my mother when she was little, with
her own mother, Rebecca, and her two brothers,
Charles and Franck. They posed under a sycamore
tree, usually the three children in descending order
of size or with Rose in front of Franck, him with
both hands on her shoulders as if to say, she's mine,
her curly hair is mine, her yellow eyes are mine, and
so are her dress, her ankles, and her bare feet. I had

swiped the magnifying glass, which cohabitated with forks and teaspoons in the kitchen drawer, and I poured over those images, trying to make out Rose's features, and more particularly, to see what she looked like at my ages with hair and eyebrows— I was tempted to wonder whether I would lose my hair and eyebrows at the same age as her (was it sixteen?) and whether I absolutely had to discover the circumstances of her martyrdom so that I could avoid analogous situations.

When Rebecca the mother posed beside them I wondered, did the father take these pictures before his helicopter-borne disappearance or a friend, or rather more simply or more accurately, had she braved the self-timer, run over to them, straightened her clothes, scraped a stray curl behind her ear, and smiled with her offspring so that one day her granddaughter could sit on a terrace in Camerone trying to identify her mother in these pictures with their faded colors, or at least identify a sort of foreknowledge that her mother would disappear someday, something in Rose's eyes that would already have said, one day I will vanish into thin air.

—

Mr. Loyal stayed with me, hovering between the living room and the terrace, every now and then he would come up to see me with a tub of ice cream in each hand and metal spoons flashing brilliantly in

69

the sunlight. We looked at the pictures of mom, filling ourselves with the frozen milky substance, feeling it creeping into our darkest depths, tracking its progress through our intimate passages. I remember the little bench and the cushions and the sun sinking abruptly into the sea, my father saying, is it good, my cricket? and I would mumble something, and we would stay there, incapable of further conversation, incapable of revealing to each other either the effect her absence had on us deep inside or the whimsical explanations we had for her leaving.

Sometimes I thought, I don't speak the same language as him, we can't talk, then the thought that I hadn't spoken the same language as mom either would make me suddenly sad.

—

On the eighth evening, confronted with his silence (which I was no better at penetrating than my mother's on the subject of her tortured scalp), I wanted to give my father a key to mom's disappearance, so while we were sitting in front of the TV (our favorite film, both of us, was Frank Capra's *It's a Wonderful Life*), intertwined, me lying down with my head on his impressive stomach and my feet in the air, swinging my putty-colored sandals on the tips of my toes, him sprawled, deflated like a wind sock without a whisper of a breeze, when we were comfortable in the muffled shadows of the living room, I said, in a nasal voice because of the position I was in, a voice even I hardly recognized as my own, I told him, she didn't leave of her own free will. I left a measured pause, then added sententiously, otherwise she would have taken the photos of me.

Mr. Loyal didn't respond. He let out a soft sigh, delicate as a sparrow.

———

We could try to get someone to look for her, I told my father, we could call the police.

He shook his head, we have to leave her alone, you have to give the people you love the right to disappear.

I scowled. It wasn't that simple, I reasoned with myself, something terrible could have happened to her, maybe she'd lost her memory and was wandering around service plazas on the freeway and couldn't even remember her own name. Perhaps she'd been clinging to life in some hospital for weeks, unable to utter a single word, the connections short-circuited in her precious brain.

When my father answered the phone he said she had gone back to her mother for a while, that was what he said: she's gone back to her mother for a while, she needed some quiet, but what did that "while" mean, and who was my mother's mother? I'd never met her, was she still alive? and where have mom's friends gone, I wondered, the ones who came in the evening when Mr. Loyal wasn't here, did they disappear at the same time, did they go off along the coast in a minibus, singing and whistling, and heading for the border?

You ought to go and apologize to Mrs. Isis, he eventually suggested. Her canary died in all this.

I didn't answer, I couldn't really see how I could go to Mrs. Isis and ask for her absolution for my suicide attempt that had cost the life of her feathered friend.

He insisted, I could come with you if you like.

Which seemed even worse to me.

I avoided it for a while, completely preoccupied with my father's response to Mommy Rose's disappearance.

I persuaded myself that mom had simply become invisible, dissolving into the perfect evening air when I was still in the hospital. I already had intimate knowledge of disappearances—the letters that no longer appear on the typewriter because the ink roll is definitively sterile and dry, the things you lose and never see again, mom used to talk about a vanishing hole because I so often complained that I couldn't find a particular toy or a book or a diamante headband, and mom would say that they had gone into the vanishing hole, according to her there was a hole that formed in the middle of the living room and swallowed our things and then closed up again. Once there, in that hole, things would start living a new life, a free and happy life, which meant that when something disappeared it was cause for celebration, mom was always keen to persuade me of that, I would mooch around for a while, despairing at my loss, but eventually resigned myself to believing in her wonderful fable.

I left my father to his apathy—rum raisin ice cream and beer—and I concentrated my efforts on trying to reach those invisible territories to which people disappear to have fun till the end of time.

THIRTEEN

IN THE END I WENT TO SEE MRS. ISIS. Not to apologize at all—although that was the pretext for my visit—and not to justify myself at all—don't you see, Mrs. Isis, I had this uncontrollable urge to fly in my pink and black cape—no, I went to see her because Mrs. Isis knew who mommy was.

Mrs. Isis, it seemed to me, had a link with secret worlds, I even suspected she had some contact with the dead (she spoke fluently to her husband who was long gone). And she knew who Mommy Rose was.

I didn't know whether they had talked together much or whether she had known mom when she was just a little girl with hair that was real hair. But I was counting on her to set some order in this mysterious assortment of stitches that would eventually form the pattern of the tapestry.

She lived three floors down from our apartment, she wore nylon blouses featuring interlocking geometric shapes that created optical illusions: is

Mrs. Isis far away, is she near, is she concave or convex? I knew she put forty-seven hairpins in her hair every morning, scrupulously counting them every evening and searching about on all fours for any that were missing from the roll call, and she did have a topknot that defied gravity—it was Mr. Loyal who said that, Mrs. Isis's topknot defies gravity. It was red and a good thirty centimeters high and it looked like whisked egg whites (except not white ones), she lacquered it copiously using asphyxiating hair spray and dropped little particles of glue wherever she went all day long.

I had always really liked Mrs. Isis.

I called her Nice Mrs. Isis.

Because of me and my rather brash despair—there was something trivial about jumping from a window in a cape—Mrs. Isis was now in mourning for her squashed canary.

But she didn't hold it against me.

She just said, it was a pretty ordinary suicide, that was what she told me as she hand-washed her geometric blouses in the kitchen sink. She turned toward me and took me to task, look at you, Rosa Rosa Rosa, look at you, you're fat as a winter sardine, you're all little and soft and round, you're so little you look like a seven-year-old, oh no, Rosa, you shouldn't be thinking about things like that at your age, and don't go telling Mrs. Isis you fell and it wasn't on purpose, no, no, my Rosa Rosa, don't go doing that kind of thing again, that only leads to unhappiness, such unhappiness (she closed her eyes, her thoughts dedicated to her little Sisi).

I nodded in agreement, thinking, she's exaggerating, I don't look like a seven-year-old, and I promised myself: I'll ask at the Institute if I really look like a little girl, they'll know, they've got points of reference. And while she kept saying, don't go doing that again, Rose, or you'll make everyone unhappy, I couldn't stop wondering how a girl my age could look like such a tiny kid, I wondered what sort of illness I had, what had misfired in my genetic inheritance, what atavistic shortcomings my organs harbored (DNA molecules that were overweight and short of breath?). I wasn't seven years old, I was more than twice that.

I had gone to see Mrs. Isis on the eleventh day.

I had knocked on her door, jumped up with both feet so that she could see me through her peephole—ah, Mrs. Isis's peephole!—waved my arms and cried, it's Rose from the eighth floor, and when she opened the door I presented her with a tray of madeleine cookies (with candied orange peel) that we had made for her, daddy and me, and that I had carried down to her, stopping every three steps to pick up the odd one tumbling down the stairs. Mrs. Isis acted as if she thought it was quite normal for me to come and apologize for my irresponsible behavior—but what did they honestly expect of me?—and to buy her indulgence with orange-flavored madeleines. I quickly got the formality over with, sorry, sorry, Mrs. Isis, I don't know how to make you forgive me, I'm so sorry your little Sisi is dead, and she stood there simpering for a moment with the tray of madeleines in her hand, eventually inviting me into her apartment, stay for a while, my Rose, we'll talk, I could do with a talk, it'll be relaxing, you know, it's not at all the same without Sisi.

So I trotted along behind her, went into the kitchen, sat down on a rush-seated chair in my pink shorts—not a skirt, never a skirt, that's too girlie, too scary—letting my legs swing and sniffing and fiddling with the seventy little braids I had on my head, and I said to her: I'd really like to go see daddy's circus.

She burst out laughing, Mrs. Isis did. A circus, a circus, you call that a circus? and the egg whites (which weren't white) quivered and threatened to create an avalanche. She turned to face me—she was making her first coffee of the day— and asked, who made all those braids for you? I told her it was a summer hairstyle, that I would have to take them out to go back to the Institute, that I would end up with a great mop of hair like a mad woman but that didn't matter given that everyone at the Institute was crazy. She shook her head and said, come on, come on, then leaned against the sink and looked out the window, sipping her coffee sweetened with caramel, and said, it's not really a circus, you know, where your father works. For a moment I shut down the hatches, thinking, if it isn't a circus, what am I going to call my father, how am I going to refer to him, seeing as I always call him the circus manager. This is revelations day, I told myself, and I suddenly felt stifled in there, it was all going too quickly for me, I wasn't totally ready yet, I said very clearly, could we go out someplace? Mrs. Isis raised an eyebrow, aren't you going to the Institute? Are you sure? I explained that I wasn't going back till the next day and that in the meantime I'd really like to go eat some fish with her for lunch in the little student restaurant she took us to once (in the days before mom disappeared) opposite the strip of wasteland. She said that the students had mostly gone, that only the ones who failed their exams in the spring were left, but that it was a good idea, that they would all be tanned and not as hyper as usual, and yes, why not, in fact, that way we won't come across the tourists you get on the seafront, the ones who wear baggy shorts and plastic shoes and couldn't give a damn that this beach isn't a real beach.

I waited in the kitchen while she got ready.

I looked around. There were thousands of things

in butterfly shapes: place mats, refrigerator magnets, the tulle lampshade on the overhead light, the salt-cellar and the pepper mill it was snuggled close to like a lover, sequined stickers on the wardrobe, there were butterflies everywhere. It was a funny idea, living with so many butterflies around, it started me thinking, would Mrs. Isis have liked to metamorphose into a huge butterfly with quivering tubular antennae and geometric patterns on her wings?

She came back and we set off arm in arm. Mrs. Isis walked very slowly, breathing hard and chirping on about Mr. Isis and the job he allegedly did in a clinic where they cured memory problems—there are some people, she said, who have such bad memories they can't remember where they've parked their cars or even, in more serious cases, people who have gaps in their memories, gaps about their childhood (exactly who were my parents?) or their marriage (who on earth is this guy next to me, snoring?). Mrs. Isis says she worked as a medical secretary in this memory clinic, she told me anecdotes about the patients—the man who lost his prosthetic arm, who couldn't remember whether he ever actually had one or why he was missing an arm, the woman who could no longer read her own name...

I didn't believe a word she told me. I knew that her husband, Mr. Isis, who had been dead many

years, had incinerated animals in a vivisection labo-
ratory. But I think that the deceased's job was so
horrible that she needed to produce these wily concoctions to nurture her memory of him.

It was mommy who had told me (but don't
breathe a word!) the truth about the late Mr. Isis.

We eventually reached the student restaurant
opposite the wasteland, with its cactus vegetation
and its dried-out shrubs, which crumbled between
your fingers with an autumnal little noise. We sat at
a table near the window so that we had a good view
of the street and the wasteland, so we could watch
the girl in the red shorts sitting on the carcass of an
old car, sipping something from a cardboard cup
and screwing up her eyes (me thinking, why doesn't
that pretty girl in the red shorts wear sunglasses?).
We ate our battered fish in silence, I listened to the
students talking around us, to their stories about
love and lust, their little jobs, the price of boots in
Harry's store, stuff to do with piercings, teachers,
money, hair bleach, life. Mrs. Isis smiled at me and
said, if you watch your step you could be like them
when you grow up. I thought about "watching my
step," it meant no suicide attempts, no tantrums
(belching, drooling, falling down paralyzed, peeing
on the floor, oh, that pool getting bigger and bigger,
the burning on my thighs, the wanting to hold on to
everything and then no, letting it all go, giving up,

the pool getting bigger like it's spelling out my shortcomings in big flashing letters, my poor girl, my poor little girl, you need someone to clean you up, to scour you and perfume you, otherwise the smell of pee, the sticky pee that I can't get rid of, seeping into my nostrils and my throat, I stop breathing, feel the pins and needles under my scalp, imminent collapse, the rush of anger that takes my legs from under me like a subterranean current, how could I "watch my step"?).

I told Mrs. Isis that mom had disappeared before I even came out of the hospital, she nodded because she already knew, or to show me that she was really listening, she sucked her fingers because of the salt and oil, drank her beer, patted her geometric bosom—I could use special glasses to see Mrs. Isis's dress, green and red glasses so I could see it properly in 3-D—she leaned over to me, I know, I know, my little jackrabbit, and tell me, my pretty one, do you have any idea where she is now? I dropped the corners of my mouth and shrugged my shoulders to stop myself from crying and to get Mrs. Isis to give me some clues. She said, your mom's quite an unusual lady but I just can't believe she would leave without saying something to me. I realized that I didn't really know the true terms of the relationship between my mother and this Mrs. Isis. I told her the story of the newspaper, which, according to me, had triggered her disappearance. She said, that's easy, easy, I must still have it at home, we can look through it. That was when I felt I could put my sadness into this woman's hands, place it gently in the crook of her hand, just having to check that it was trickling smoothly between the gaps in her fingers like fine sand, a finite amount of powdered seashell. I gave out a long sigh like a hot air balloon touching down.

We left the student restaurant, Mrs. Isis took a moment to light a cigarette, and we walked home slowly, crossing backward and forward over the street to stay in the shade, hugging the walls of the buildings, scuttling one behind the other in some places to avoid the risk of sunstroke (when we crossed the street, I felt we were leaving ourselves exposed to a possible sniper waiting in ambush because she looked anxiously from left to right then dead ahead, tottering over to the sheltered territory with all the urgency and fear of a soldier wading through the swamps before getting back to the safety of his trench).

Once back in her butterfly-filled apartment she started rummaging through her cupboard of newspapers—for rereading when there was time, for wrapping up the potato peelings, and rereading while she was at it, peeler held in midair while she focused all her attention on an article she had missed during her first consultation—she asked me several times to confirm the date, and I was completely absorbed by the spectacle of all those butterflies around me (tapestry cushions, macramé place mats, plastic butterflies scattered about a rubber plant, multicolored insects pinned through the abdomen onto a dusty velvet background with their common names written in italic script on suitable labels: *Lesser Purple Emperor, Orange Tip, Northern Brown, Two-Tailed Pasha, Brown Argus*), imagining them sniggering, all those butterflies sniggering at the sight of us leaning toward each other on that dazzling afternoon, her trying to find the one thing that would help me move farther along the embankment or would arrest my obscure desire to follow its smooth curve.

In the end she produced the paper in question from inside the cupboard with a triumphant flourish, it was already a little yellowed with that slight staleness of something ephemeral that has had the temerity to last. I said, right, what do we do now? She frowned. I let her choose what direction operations should take. She sat down at the table in the living room, beginning her inspection with the News in Brief section, with me sitting next to her trying to take part in the inspection but not succeeding in identifying what I was looking for, my eye alighting on everything and anything, achieving nothing, thrown by all those columns of print, so many of them I wouldn't know how to find what might have interested my mother, and then Mrs. Isis stood up suddenly, sighing and pointing at a short article and saying, that's it, that was it, and me, kneeling on a chair, leaning closer to see and reading the piece: Markus M. tried to commit suicide with a jump rope in his cell on the eve of his appeal, and me not really understanding, and all I could do was wonder, why would guys in prison have jump ropes in their cells? mulling the question over intently, and Mrs. Isis watching me out of the corner of her eye with a painful grimace on her face, and me eventually asking her, what do they need jump ropes for, the guys in prison? only wanting an answer to that question for now, unable to contemplate her replying to anything else, targeting the problem, and, I hoped, intimating that I wanted her to give me a precise answer to that precise question.

PART TWO

FOURTEEN

MARKUS M. LIVED WITH HIS MOTHER in a sort of mobile home in the heights of Milena near the artificial lake. It was a construction that didn't bear up very well to its sedentary situation or the rigors of winter. It had partly collapsed, rather like the opening to a mine or a slag heap of sand, putting up little resistance to the bad weather or the moisture progressing along a subterranean route through layers of rock, leading down to the lake, which was now teeming with catfish. These fish had decimated the rest of the aquatic population with such application that, as a child, Markus M. was afraid the predatory creatures would make their way up from the lake all the way to their trailer through the groundwater network and gobble them up, him and his mother, in their sleep.

Markus M. often wondered why he lived with his mother in a mobile home when other children lived in brick houses covered in plaster, he often wondered what had driven his mother to prefer the less-than-remote possibility of ever leaving to the relative security of a house made of crates and pallets.

Because of his mother, who had something of the old hell-raising agitator about her (four-square and solitary), who dyed her hair an unequivocal blond, often complaining about cowardly men with poor judgment who slept with skinny, barely pubescent girls; because of his mother, who whined in front of the TV when tanned, slick-haired, epilated boys abandoned their girlfriends; because of his mother, then, who never managed to earn his respect—didn't even try to anymore now—because she was a waitress, smoked strong cigarettes, talked in a throaty voice, and practiced a versatile sexuality; because of all these factors, Markus felt constrained to finish high school in order to spend as little time as possible in Milena (the high school was in the neighboring town) in the hopes that, when it was over, he would find some other job than working in the gold mine, and as soon as he had his qualifications under his belt, he would be on his way. At the end of the day, Markus M. was a sensible boy.

Markus wanted to leave the area as soon as was feasible but he felt shackled by his own inertia. He loved those coniferous mountains, that cold air breathing through his body like a foghorn, he was overawed by the ravaged rock formations, the prehistoric intimacy he enjoyed with the scree slopes, the noise of the open mine and the cyanide-blue pools, the smell of diesel and decay that sometimes hung over the town because the wind stagnated in this enclave, Markus M. stamped his feet so that his blood would circulate and not dawdle too long on its internal circuit, Markus M. counted the magpies over the railway footbridge, one for sorrow, two for joy, three I'm right back where I started, Markus M. was a melancholy boy just going through the motions, a melancholy boy just looking the part.

I'm looking at Markus M. from where I'm standing.

Markus M., he's the sort of boy I like.

I think about him now, now that I know he has attempted suicide in a prison in the middle of a town I have never set foot in...

I think about him and I see him as dirty and beautiful, and soft as something that comes out of a bread bin, something precious, something you would nestle in sawdust to stop it from breaking. From now on I'll think of Markus M. when I feel isolated in cold, snowy wastes, when I feel and look as if I'm seven years old (when I'm actually more than twice that). I like picturing what happened to Markus M. and my mother.

All this is connected to my mother's childhood, but what can I do with my mother's childhood?

what can I even dare to understand about such a mystery? My father's childhood feels more imaginable to me because it's straight out of a novel. I can put what I want into it, arrange the events and people's thoughts however I please, pick through it to find proof and explanations, plug the gaps to stop my submarine from sinking, I can invent a childhood for him, and a continuous ribbon of thoughts, no one can stop me.

FIFTEEN

I WENT BACK TO THE INSTITUTE ON THE TWELFTH DAY. I played the game, answered the questions, ate the cracked wheat and the polyurethane ham, which makes a sort of rainbow if I tilt the plate the right way, I always think, they make it with kerosene or motor oil, I went back to class, didn't talk much, smiled when I had to, and sweated discreetly with no smell and no trickling, it was so hot at the Institute I thought about candles melting, languishing and melting at the height of summer, I was better and more brilliant than the others—but I knew I was like a sighted person among the blind, it was nothing to do with more profound qualities—I dreamed about the rain and the pine forests my mother and father had known, imagining the sound of the rain making a sort of wall of noise, a white wall of sibilant sound, I didn't say that mom had disappeared, and Mr. Loyal didn't mention it to them either, which seriously confirmed my doubts, in the end they called me into the education office, the guy in white, Mr. Roberto, asked me without really asking me, would you be able to walk home by yourself? your father said that you could walk home by yourself now (he waved a letter that I had brought in that same morning), if you're frightened, if you'd rather stay for a bit, we'll call him and we'll explain, I said, no, of course I'm not frightened, why would I be scared, you know how old I am, and then I laid it on a bit, I often go down to the beach all on my own, anyway. I often go to Swordfish Beach to swim, but he didn't believe me, I just said, you know how old I am, again, but it didn't seem to impress him at all, so I stopped lying, he smiled, he was bored with me, I could see he was bored, I felt like patting him gently on the shoulder and I was upset that I was boring this person, I thought of Mr. Loyal, she can walk home on her own, I thought of mom and her sugary wig, then I brought a halt to my inadequate thoughts, put on my sensible face, and said, I can walk home on my own, don't worry, I'm fine.

He stood up in his white coat, you'd better go home and look after your rabbits, I kept my knees tightly together, my hands perfectly encompassing their roundedness, this guy didn't know mom had disappeared, I smiled, taking special care to be symmetrical, I wanted the left-hand side of my body to be the exact inverse of the right-hand side. I nodded, in a measured way, tilting my chin right down till it touched my neck. You go home now and look after your rabbits.

SIXTEEN

For a long time Markus M. believed he didn't like women.

He couldn't bear his mother touching him, and the disgust he felt for her was disturbing. He very vaguely remembered—but the memory wafted to him like a bad smell—that he must have loved her as a child, he must have wanted to snuggle up on her lap, occasionally he would remember a woolen sweater that scratched his cheeks slightly, and his mother's breasts beneath the woolen sweater, but there was nothing left of the sensation, only the slight unease that its exhumation provoked. His mother's smell put him off because of the mint candy she sucked on—with a lot of lip-smacking—to help her digest, because of her talc, and because of the scent (Underwood, it was called) she sprayed over him in the small hours when he was little and had rushed to the Port-a-potty to be sick (something he did with the sort of regularity required by an additional bodily function), but also because of the acid tang of her lipstick, which she left on the mouths of bottles; the sweat from her armpits, which she didn't shave to prove that she really was an ex-blond; her girl's tobacco, fine and filtered; her fabric conditioner, the hair conditioner that went with her shampoo, the smell of her laddered and darned pantyhose, her purple underwear—women who live in mobile homes only wear purple underwear, although they call it damson-colored lingerie—the smell of burned fat clinging to her hair and her scarves, her flabby upper arms, elbows, and buttocks (Markus thinks everyone notices his mother's smells, and that's why no one in Milena talks to her with anything other than condescension, while keeping a hygienic distance—don't come any closer than that—apart from, it goes without saying, the Lucies, Maries, and Yvonnes who wear purple underwear like her and complain that all men are weak). At one point Markus M. wondered whether this revulsion he felt for her wasn't hiding something more pernicious, which made him lie awake at night with his hand on his dick trying to conjure up images of girls with tits and asses, girls he knew or passed in silence, something that made a voice in a tiny corner of his brain keep at him with the insistence of a migraine, saying, maybe you're a fag, Markus, maybe you prefer guys. And he no longer knew whether it was this constantly repeated question that made him go limp or whether the virtual wiggling of those tits-and-ass girls genuinely didn't stir his blood at all.

So Markus M. spent most of his time sprawled on his bed—his mother had been sleeping on the sofa for ages because she came home late from the cafeteria, and she thought he needed his privacy. She would pop her head around the door, look at him with her brown eyes (she said, they're hazel, or if there was some sunlight she would even say, they're green), and ask if he would like anything to eat. Markus didn't look at her, he was just sad he could never overcome the revulsion that contaminated everything she brought home, she came over to him and he felt like a hare in the bottom of its burrow, trapped by a fire, she leaned over to pick up some dirty washing—and he saw the top of her G-string peeping above her jeans, and the thought of his mother in a G-string with her ridiculous little tattoos on her buttocks overwhelmed him, overpowered him. She didn't know what to do to hold on to this son of hers who seemed to be slipping away from her so fast, the image it suggested to her was a comet in the very depths of a black sky, that was how she imagined her Markus, hurtling away, leaving in his wake microscopic splinters of light from his stolen sneakers. Still, she smiled and told herself,

he'll come back to me in the end, he'll come back—
because, unlike him, she did know that he had been
a wonderful, gentle child, a soft, protective boy who
stroked her hair when she cried and sang songs to
her. So she would just remind him that she had
brought home some chicken stew with olives and
that before she went on duty today she was going
out with Marie—or Lucie or Agathe or any other
divorced woman with a couple of kids and a car and
a job, a proper job, hairdresser, beautician, or
nursery nurse. Markus would nod, with his head
still on the pillow, and he would say, close the door
behind you, and his mother—whose own name was
Marie or Lucie or Agathe—feeling she had been dis-
missed, would leave her son's bedroom with the
words *see you later, pet*, and him opening one eye
and realizing how violently he loathed her with her
I'm-the-victim-here attitude and her straggly hair
and because he couldn't find the way back to her
anymore.

SEVENTEEN

I STARTED SUSPECTING MR. LOYAL on the twentieth day.

It was like a sort of resin. Something that started seeping stickily on my hands, with a flattering amber color at first but eventually darkening until it was an utterly black glue. I didn't know what to do with my suspicions.

I just started watching him, looking out for any false moves, an intonation that would betray him, a spiteful glint in his eye, anything in fact that would prove to me that he was guilty.

I watched him attentively.

I'm very gifted at keeping watch like that.

He'll go back to the place he strangled her eventually, I told myself. Then I pushed the thought aside, flushing to think I could nurture that sort of suspicion.

But it was no good, his intimate relationship with secrecy, the facility he had for evicting potential visitors (telephone inquiries and unfortunate people on the doorstep sent packing), the ease with which he told them, she's with her mother, while he gnawed at the thumbnail of his right hand, making the flesh around the nail bleed very slightly, then licking it, sucking on it with a little slurping sound while he strung them along and lied to them, doing it casually without any panache or flair, just using realistic little lies, untruths that seemed like the truth, the way he accepted her absence so lightly, and ultimately, his inability to construct plausible scenarios for her disappearance with me; all this necessarily encouraged me to see him as the main suspect, the first and only one on my list.

I watched him searching through the freezer for ice cream, and I walked behind him, waiting until he had shut himself in the bathroom before climbing onto a chair, lifting the lid of the freezer, and trying to extricate the plastic bags, which were no longer translucent in their frozen state, so that I could examine their contents, rummaging through the icy depths of the machine, nosing around for a clue, a solidified piece of my mother, a vaguely human shape, but that cenotaph contained nothing but skinned rabbits and tubs and tubs of vanilla ice cream.

I dug little holes in the walls with the point of my compass so that I could overhear his telephone conversations in case he had an accomplice.

When we sat down in the half-light of the living room to watch our favorite films—the dream life of black-and-white films from the '50s, the perfection of that gloriously lit cardboard world, Clark Gable, James Stewart, Gregory Peck, sets streaming past a motionless car, zero risk—I chose Hitchcock to monitor his reactions to the stories of murder, glasses of poisoned milk, blood-soaked showers, serial lying, and double-crossing.

I remembered his episodic jealousy about mom's friends, the few scenes I had witnessed, but there was no material there for murderous rage.

Still I persisted.

I set traps for him.

I would sit opposite him so that I could really see his face and spot the slightest questionable sign of tension, and I would say something like, I think she must have been wearing her red shoes, I can't find them anywhere (thinking that, if he really had got rid of her, he probably wouldn't have forgotten what shoes the body was wearing, hoping that he would look up and say, no, not her red shoes, she wasn't wearing her red shoes…), but he would just grunt something that alternated between his disapproval of my systematic search through mom's belongings and his indulgence toward what he saw as my distress at her disappearance…

I was floundering.

I went down to see Mrs. Isis to hear her talk about mom.

I was floundering.

Later, and this seemed like a logical extension, I started to worry that he would strangle me too.

—

One time, it must have been on the twenty-seventh day, when he was in the bathroom for his morning ablutions, with the radio sitting on the basin whispering and spluttering quietly, I posted myself outside the door to spy on him. Cool air was filtering through the keyhole like cold milk and it hurt my eye, I got used to it, rubbing my eye, settling back into my spying position with my ass in the air, leaning forward, my hands on my knees, him fat and pink on the far side of the door, with too much skin and flesh, a white towel around his waist, and his breasts hanging over his stomach, the curve of his biceps and his belly, the gentle, absent look in his eye—yes, that was it, a gentle, absent expression, that was it, a sort of well-meaning indifference— when he looked in the mirror on the little medicine cabinet above the basin, he was shaving, his face was covered in immaculate white mousse, I noticed as I looked for clues, for any compromising gesture, and he was still lost in the white noise produced by his shambling radio, probably thinking of his better days, before my mother perhaps, casting back to sweet memories related to his childhood—Mr. Loyal as a fat little boy in a sailor suit, left hand mommy, right hand daddy, smiling, framed by these big kind parents—probably thinking, what in God's name am I doing here with crazy Rose in this apartment that's falling to pieces, what the hell am I doing here? or maybe he wasn't thinking anything, given that Mr. Loyal only very rarely emerged from his pachyderm neutrality, smiling at himself in the mirror, because he liked the look of himself or he regretted it, or just because somewhere behind the cascading noise from the basin he could hear the morons, the crooners, and the idiots chuckling to each other inside his radio, Mr. Loyal was smiling lingeringly to himself, and that smile suddenly started to worry me, that smile that I now interpreted as evil, his little canines stick out over his lips, I thought, I'm scared of Mr. Loyal, he could have every intention of fattening me up—and I thought of the ice cream and the pastries—and gobbling me up when I reach the required size, that must be why he's always buried in recipe books, so that he can find the most appropriate one for my flavor, stuffed quail, casseroled Rose, prepare it well and serve it up, or perhaps he's going to abuse me (abuse, abuse, abuse, mom would have said, what do you mean by that?), fiddle with me, touch me up, rape me, force me to lick him and fondle him. I was suddenly overwhelmed with fear. I could already see the headlines, having strangled the mother, he sodomizes the daughter, I went crazy, backing away and trotting barefoot over the wooden floor, looking for a possible escape route, I headed for the front door, it was double locked, which for me at that point had nothing to do with nocturnal necessity in Camerone (the junkies who threatened you with a syringe every night, the networks of thugs in the stairwell…) but had everything to do with my father's wish to keep me for his private consumption, all to himself, all for him, I looked closely at the door, where are the keys? I looked closely at the door, I felt helpless, I didn't know where those fucking keys were, I spun around, at the end of the corridor I could hear the tubercular radio from the bathroom, I went into the kitchen and took everything out from under the sink—bleach, plastic bags, suffocating aerosols—to make a space for myself where I could disappear, there really had to be some way I could shift into a parallel dimension in this house, and if there was a door into these unknown territories, you definitely had to head for the space under the sink, that was obvious, it was the darkest place in the house and the smelliest (a strong poisonous smell), I contemplated the effects of my panic, I had hurled everything messily onto the tiled floor, cleaning products, wax polish, and cloths, Mr. Loyal would know straight away that I was hiding under there, so I gave up, and turned back around, I had to disappear, I went into the living room telling myself, I must get to the terrace, at least I'll be with my rabbits, except that to get to the terrace I have to go out onto the landing, I don't have the keys, he must have them in the pocket of his pants folded on the stool in the bathroom, so I opened the window, I started my whole stupid performance again, I climbed out the window, jumped down onto the sill, there was a ledge all the way along the building, a ledge that was a good thirty centimeters wide, that was enough for me, I was a tiny round ball and I didn't suffer from vertigo, it was windy on that ledge, every gust set up awful eddies that wrapped themselves around me, I was up on that ledge in my shorts and I didn't have my cape, I was just trying to get away from Mr. Loyal and his gluttony, I didn't tell myself that people would see me from down below, they never looked up, and if the idea ever did cross their minds, I would be invisible to them because of the muddle of blinds and rococo oddities on the façade of the building, I stood there frozen for a moment to get used to the wind, I wasn't frightened, I was just trying to find a comfortable position, I was on the north face, it was terribly cold, the tips of my fingers were freezing, I was wearing pink shorts, a sleeveless top with sexy-girl sequins, and ankle socks—

bunched around my ankles to avoid that ridiculous look when they are pulled up the calves—I had sandals with nonslip rubber soles, which were being put to full use now, I was in pink shorts on the ledge of the north face, I walked along the ledge toward the corner of the building, toward the light, toward the east, I reached the corner, I didn't look down at the palm trees, the blinds, the Lilliputians, the gleaming cars, I clasped the corner with both arms, I managed not to look down, I was in control of the situation, hugging the stone, I was sure I wouldn't have the strength to climb up to the terrace, I didn't really know how I would have gone about it anyway, because there was no fire escape or safety ladder, I ended up on the east face, the light was fierce there and it warmed the tips of my fingers, I was sheltered from the wind now, it was hot and bright, I'm going to stay here for a while, I told myself and sat down on ledge, dangling my legs, feeling slightly intoxicated, I thought of Mr. Loyal, who would soon be coming out of the bathroom, short-sleeved shirt and white linen trousers, appropriate integrity, beautifully ironed, he would call me, in fact I could already hear him, Rose, Rosita, my Rose, he would look for me, stand perplexed by the locked front door, search through the house, panic, he would look out the living room window (which I had left open) to check that I hadn't jumped again, he would

lean out to make absolutely sure a gathering hadn't
formed on the sidewalk around my broken little
body, all pink-red and white, he would grab the
phone and call Mrs. Isis, asking against all logic,
Rosie's not with you, is she? and she would reassure
him, she would say, she must be on the terrace, you
must have locked the door again without realizing,
him shaking his head, no, no, that's not possible, but
going out onto the landing all the same, soon joined
by Mrs. Isis, they would go up to the terrace together,
they would start getting seriously worried, and then,
at that point in my projections, I no longer really
knew why I was on the ledge and what I was so
afraid of, now Mr. Loyal seemed nothing more or
less than a rather sentimental and melancholy step-
father who meant me no harm at all, I heard his
voice and the concern strangling it slightly, I shuf-
fled back against the façade, stood up, and went
back to the north face, taking tiny steps, I jumped in
through the window and trotted into the kitchen,
where I made myself some toast with jam, I waited
for Mrs. Isis and Mr. Loyal to come back down from
the terrace, neither of them managing to formulate
their alarm, and what if she's gone disappeared
evaporated like her mother? I waited for them to
come back down, devastated to have lost me, they
came into the kitchen and saw me sitting at the
table, yellow checkered tablecloth, wisteria twisting

its way between the little vinyl squares, sliced bread
and red currant jelly, me with the tiniest hint of
cruel pleasure seeing them so confused, Mr. Loyal
filling the entire doorway, Mrs. Isis trying to get a
glimpse, saying, is she there? is she there, then? and
him sincerely wondering whether he was losing the
plot, while I put myself in the witness stand and
asked myself, am I really that perverse? am I such a
nasty little girl? pitying him now that he looked so
pitiful, then sighing and knowing that—either
way—my mind would start whirring again the very
next day and I'd be inventing horrible scenarios and
going down to be with Mrs. Isis to try and see some
clarity in the immeasurable loss I had felt since
mom disappeared.

EIGHTEEN

WHEN SHE WAS A GIRL, long before she met my father, Markus, and their lives took this bad turn, Rose went to school in the little brick building attached to the town hall in Milena. Every morning Franck, brother number two, would take her right to the door of the school. He refused to acknowledge that she could have gone on her own. He always took her too early because, after dropping her off, he set off for the gold mine—the Site, they all called it—and you really couldn't be late getting to the Site. Charles would already be there, the foreman hated anyone being late, he would go completely red in the face and yell and breathe so hard you thought scalding steam might come out of his ears—like it came out of bulls' nostrils in Rose's cartoons—and eventually he would take your name off the time sheets as a result of your accumulated failures (daily checks of late arrivals and random checks of your alcohol level) and you would have nowhere left to go, you had to leave Milena or to choose another job that didn't pay so well, if you really wanted to stay in Milena to watch little Rose's comings and goings.

So Franck dropped Rose off much too early, he left her in the schoolyard, under the chestnut trees (with their iron fences protecting their roots and that little area of soil from the invading blacktop), and Rose would think to herself, under the blacktop there is mud, and there's clay and gold and compost, there are moles and worms, a whole mysterious underground life, there are bones and fossils, bodies and mice. Rose was all by herself in the yard, so it was quite natural for her to be thinking about bodies and worms and their subterranean trafficking. At first she had run about, skipped with her rope and played hopscotch, but in the end she lost the urge to fill that monstrous expanse of space, she would sit under the stunted limbs of a chestnut tree and read comic books, already nibbling at her lunch and—to justify that premature nibbling—muttering, well, it's inside now and whether it's in now or in two hours' time, I can't really see the difference, eating her salami and mortadella, tugging at the previous day's bread with her teeth because it had developed an elastic quality in the night, biting into her apple and her small square of dark chocolate, soon replete, long before the other children arrived, relieved of the chore of eating, free for the day ahead.

—

At four o'clock Franck took a break, went to pick Rose up from school, quickly ran her home on his bike—Rose sitting on the luggage rack, perpendicular to the road, her legs hanging down on the right-hand side of the bike, always on the right-hand side, feeling nothing but the wind playing in her hair and the jolting against her buttocks, holding tightly on to the saddle that Franck never sat his ass on—he pedaled all the way up the hill to the house, dropped Rose off, and went back down with his feet in the air, spraying up pebbles, gravel, and snail shells, splattering everyone, and muttering, quick, quick through clenched teeth, getting back to the Site, where he worked a little later than all the others because of the break he had taken, teased by his fellow workers (your Rose won't break, you know) but smiling, smiling at Charles and all the others who worked at the gold mine, carrying on stubbornly, tilting his obstinate bovine forehead, happy now that he knew Rose was safe at home, not listening to the sarcastic remarks, still smiling, relieved until the next day, watched by Charles, who wouldn't dare upset him, who wouldn't dare disturb his stolid ruminations, and who eventually shrugged his shoulders, until the siren started wailing, indicating the end and some respite, until Charles went off to his changing room and put his clothes back on and left while Franck stayed on alone to catch up the time he had spent protecting Rose from her invisible enemies.

NINETEEN

IT WAS NOT LONG BEFORE I THOUGHT of Mr. Loyal's
lion.

The only thing I knew for sure about Mr. Loyal's
alleged circus was that it housed a lion who lived a
peaceful life behind bars and did nothing much
apart from eating, dozing, and pacing around a bit
to limber up its pads. The lion was old and asth-
matic, it had decaying teeth and would groan all
through the night when its teeth hurt. Mr. Loyal
would say, Rufus needs to see the dentist, or Rufus
has heartburn—his comments always had something to do with Rufus's health. Mr. Loyal had
always said he kept Rufus to remind him of the old
days (when his circus really was a circus, presum-
ably), because he didn't have the heart to get rid of
him, even though he cost a fortune to feed—as the
sensible Mr. Loyal frequently pointed out to the sentimental Mr. Loyal, the two of them balancing each
other out sufficiently for their dialogue to result in

an anvil-like inertia.

When mom was still living with us, the only thing she would agree to say about Mr. Loyal's circus was that it had an old lion and that she had worked for it a long time ago. If I asked to go and see Mr. Loyal's circus, she would say, it's no place for you. Which was a pretty surprising comment in itself, but it also harbored a prohibition that I felt implied something monstrous. If I insisted and said, but I'm fifteen, mom, she would tell me, you don't look a day over half that. She would look at me kindly, softening and repeating the words, don't think about it, don't think about it, don't think about it.

So, in my docile way, I had banned myself from thinking about it for a long time.

Which means that if a furtive thought about the circus crept into my head, I would call on all my private guardians to block the exits, surrounding the unhealthy thought and suffocate it by sitting on it. Thereby eradicating the evil thought.

Not going to Mr. Loyal's circus had not bothered me.

Until mom disappeared.

When I suspected a link between this circus and mom's absence.

And when I thought of the lion.

—

It was autumn in Camerone. The air had taken on a golden glow, even the polystyrene beach and its heaps of seashells had adopted an amberlike russet light.

Summer is coming to an end, I told myself, mom hasn't come home. My father had just been stalling, putting off resolving the enigma; he still hadn't called the police, and the longer he took to inform the authorities, the more suspect his prevaricating became. She had been gone forty days now and the excuses he had cobbled together at the beginning for the man who owned the sweet shop and for her dance instructor—she's gone home to her mother—had satisfied both of them, each had gone back to his or her own preoccupations, leaving just Mrs. Isis, Mr. Loyal, and me seriously doubting that mom might reappear one day. And that doubt was excruciating—from time to time for some, but every waking moment for me.

Mr. Loyal eventually said, let's wait till December, we'll wait till Christmas, if she's not back by then, we'll let them know.

I looked at him, baffled.

To me it seemed high time we let them know already. And Christmas was still thousands of light-years away.

I was confronted by Mr. Loyal's unfathomable failure to act.

In the end I started thinking: what's Mr. Loyal going to do after Christmas? I studied the way he looked at me to find signs of weariness or disenchantment, but Mr. Loyal continued to grant me the same gentle affection. Despite all the evidence to the contrary, I carried on believing that—if he were my real father—he would be more securely attached to me through some link involving his DNA and the duplication of his cells inside my body, and that that biological evidence would have constrained him never to abandon me. The fact that he loved my now-absent mother did not strike me as substantial enough to stop the cord that bound us from fraying.

I started spending less time on the terrace, or the same amount of time but never alone; usually I was with Mrs. Isis, a well-kitted-out Mrs. Isis complete with parasol, mantilla over her shoulders, and foam rubber sandals like you would use after a bath (she must have hoped that the contact between the soles of her feet and that sponge would drain all the sweat from her body), tightly bundled into her butterflylike housecoats, and constantly sighing, there's no autumn anymore, adding quietly to herself, the leaves shrivel up and fall but we're still in this stifling heat, with a shake of her head. She took short little breaths as if carefully ventilating her body. I looked at her bra straps where they carved into her shoulders, that faded-old-underwear color, a slightly sour color associated with a fine layer of filth, indelible filth, a color that will never regain the freshness it once had and that is somehow connected to the way things die. I could spend hours looking at Mrs. Isis's bra straps, imagining the little butterfly-shaped bows and wondering about the patterns embedded into her skin, there, in the fat of her shoulders. She used to read pamphlets about domestic dangers, the risks you ran when you organized a barbecue in the woods during a heat wave with half a dozen children below the age of two under your feet. She always seemed very taken with these leaflets the local authority handed out. It was fascinating seeing her so absorbed by those highly colored inserts, the humorous illustrations, all those exclamation marks warning you against the vicissitudes of the modern world. When she wasn't immersed in the dangers she herself had avoided by not having any children and by never organizing barbecues, she would talk to me about mom, the autumn, Mr. Loyal, and Mr. Loyal's lion, and I would keep saying to myself, isn't she trying to insinuate something? Then she would come back to mom and to what she knew about the Christmases in the village where mom had lived, and I wanted to shake her, to say, make yourself clear, I don't want your insinuations, but it would have been impossible to shake her, it would have made a noise of mucous surfaces rubbing together, and the very thought of this terrifying

VÉRONIQUE OVALDÉ

noise dried my throat out. We explored the possible reasons for a voluntary departure from mom, perhaps to join Markus when he came out of prison (which could have been the ideal solution…but this hypothesis pulled itself apart because then mom wouldn't have left without any money or spare clothes, or without me…), and finally I just asked—because it was the only question I felt I was allowed to ask—I ended up asking, but if my father isn't a circus manager, what is it he manages then? and she gave a long sigh and said, just keep this under your hat, okay? I nodded, already regretting coming so close to the secrets that were tended around me like a precious garden, this is just between you and me, isn't it?, once again I earnestly nodded my agreement; she sat in silence for a few moments to heighten the effect and repeated once more—as if she owned the words—there's no autumn anymore, then eventually said, it isn't a circus, my twinkle, it isn't a circus that your father manages anymore, it's, and it has been for a long time now, it's a nude cabaret. I said nothing for a moment and then I burst out laughing. Well, what did they all take me for? Why had they been so keen to hide the truth from me all that time, did they really think I was so fragile, so out of touch with the world, so stupid that I couldn't imagine that sort of place in this town? Did they think that in my scale of possibilities a circus was a more favorable, more irreproachable, more reassuring place than a nude cabaret? I laughed until I nearly choked, Mrs. Isis was afraid I was having a breakdown; I tried to reassure her, waving one hand and saying, don't worry. When I calmed down, I just said, so mom was never a groom or an acrobat or a contortionist…and Mrs. Isis shook her head and said, how did you get ideas like that into your head, my twinkle? no, your mom met your daddy because she was looking for work and she had a pretty little ass. Reassured, Mrs. Isis gave in to a controlled fit of laughter, then she went on, she may well have been pregnant with you at the time, but there's no doubting your mother had some nerve, she must have thought, while it still doesn't show, I'll go and strip in a nude cabaret. Mrs. Isis laughed and laughed so I started laughing too, hoping this could be a happy time we spent together and she wouldn't hesitate to reveal more mysteries of our existence, I felt as if my throat were coated in plaster dust, I could hardly get the words out—let's go and get something to drink, I'm thirsty—and Mrs. Isis took me to have freshly squeezed lemon juice in the little student restaurant that we now went to regularly, and along the way I told myself, my best friend is sixty-five years old. I watched her walking a little way ahead of me, waddling like a mother duck, and I reveled in it: my best friend is sixty-five years old.

TWENTY

WHEN MR. LOYAL SAW ROSE, my mother, for the first time, he told himself, oh no, now this one must not be damaged. Because Mr. Loyal knew what happened to girls in his nude cabaret. Mr. Loyal, who had a moral code for his profession, was the sort of man who refused to have a back room at his cabaret, but he did let his girls stay on at the bar with clients after their respective performances; they would drink and make sure the johns drank, then they would abandon them at the bar or leave with one of them, and what happened after that was no longer Mr. Loyal's concern.

Mr. Loyal didn't want to know what they did with their assets, he just warned them against diseases, he spoke to them about a clean life, a healthy diet, and preserving their capital. They're grown women, anyway, he kept reminding himself. They're old enough to create their own problems and to deal with them.

Mr. Loyal was a sentimental man: for decades now he had been a team with Rufus the bouncer, who had once been the red-nosed clown in his circus, Rufus who people called "the lion" because of the sort of hair he had had before he went bald, or perhaps they said it ironically because there was nothing particularly king-of-the-beasts about him, except perhaps his way of making women work while he had brief, clandestine naps, one buttock resting on a stool and his eyes half closed as if watching everything in quiet meditation.

So when Mr. Loyal showed Rose into his office (a room with a window overlooking the courtyard but with such a dismal view that the blinds were lowered summer and winter, giving the place a rather contemplative, muted atmosphere, or per- haps it felt not unlike the bottom of a drawer in a metal filing cabinet, one that you can no longer fully open and where you may have forgotten prospec- tuses from locksmiths and cobblers, and slices of bread gone green and fluffy, something dusty, then seedy, moldy), when Rose stepped in, Mr. Loyal thought, she's a princess.

It was based on precious little, the admiration he vowed to her there and then, it was based on the contrast between the whiteness of her skin, I can see her skeleton through it, the black eyebrows drawn on in pencil to form a Roman arch, I can see her skeleton and her veins, and the blond nylon wig she wore very slightly askew, it was based on her dress, with lace and an apple-blossom print, because the girls who came to see Mr. Loyal and did their striptease routines tried to look a bit sexy from the moment they walked in, they tended toward leather trousers or studded jeans, their faces were already corrupt, and they were inclined to be tattooed, it was becoming very difficult to find a girl without some tribal filth daubed over her haunches, so seeing Rose perched on the edge of her seat in her lace-edged dress like some Amish farm girl, with those features your eye could never settle on, I can see her skin and her eyebrows, then I look at her left eye then her right eye, first the left then the right, but while I'm looking at the left eye, the right is already different, it's like the changing seasons only accelerated, Mr. Loyal thought to himself, I don't want her to be damaged, I'm going to take care of her, I think I can comfort her.

TWENTY-ONE

I WAS THE SORT WHO LIKED TO HAVE a plan B in place.

So I asked Mrs. Isis, if Mr. Loyal doesn't want me anymore, could I come and live with you? she looked amazed, she started laughing, we were in our usual little café and she was drinking her beer. She laughed very discreetly, showing her sensitivity, she had just been talking about Rufus, the lion who wasn't a lion (and I wondered, are these grown-ups going to insist on making fun of me? do they think it's funny that I believe in this story about some big cat when he's really just a bald, arthritic old doorman? do they think for one moment that if I'm told it's a lion, I picture a lion? how can they want to trick me like that?), and she said, yes, yes, don't you worry, you can come to my house, but I'm sure Mr. Loyal loves you very much anyway and wouldn't want to see you go. I thought to myself, yes, he loves me very much, just like he loves caramel-flavored ice cream, and flat-leaf parsley in his salad. So I sold the idea, you see, Mrs. Isis, I'll be leaving the Institute soon. Oh really? she said carefully, giving a little wave to the depressive waiter to get him to replace her empty glass with a full one, and I added, you see, they think I'm perfect.—Perfect, you say?—they're even wondering why I'm there, I went on, trying to ratify the point. *So,* you're better then, my love? she asked kindly. Yes, yes, I'm better, completely better. And then I really got into my stride, I'm not frightened of people anymore. I've stopped rushing to get down the stairs every morning and sneaking up on the world to catch it out when it's still all flat.—All flat? she said. And I carried on digging my hole, yes, yes, all flat, I used to think—but I don't think this anymore, of course—that the whole planet only existed when I was there, I thought—but this was when I was little, you realize that—that I was the one inventing it, so I wanted to catch the world out without its little engine, with all the people slumped on the ground like puppets and the cars going nowhere.—Going nowhere, you say?—Yes, yes, like when you press Pause when we're watching a film at your house, Mrs. Isis. I could tell I was getting out of my depth, so I went on, but that's all over and done with now, I don't shoplift anymore—So you used to shoplift? she interjected. Yes, but that's over, I used to think the whole population was employed by mom, that the security men worked for her, that the checkout girls spied on me for her when I pilfered every thing I possibly could, and everytime I emerged from the shops triumphant and unpunished, I would take comfort from that thought…— Oh, really? Is that what you were like? she asked gently. And there I was, knowing I had said too much but so desperate to confide in someone, not wanting to crush my chances of adoption but hoping I could show her clearly where I was coming from, now that things were working out well for me, there I was insisting, Mrs. Isis, the Institute is going to let me go, they've called Mr. Loyal to tell him, it's still a secret but they've let him know. Her squeezing both my hands in hers, that's wonderful, my little sweetheart, and me realizing she hadn't believed a word of my twaddle, or rather, that she doesn't believe I am cured, and incidentally isn't thinking of adopting me or adopting anything other than a serene response to my first question, that she enjoys my company and our conversations, she likes drinking beer with me and talking about mom, but that she certainly doesn't foresee ever having to live with me in her apartment. She chooses that moment to look me in the eye—with that insidious but innocent expression that she has mastered so perfectly—and to say, and, anyway, it's pretty hard for you, given that you don't have any grandparents, with your mom being an orphan.

I sit there dumbstruck. I think, mom wasn't an orphan, her father was an asshole and her mother kept chickens in Milena, mom had two brothers, I have photos to prove it. I think, what's old Isis talking about, what's she going on about? But I am quite incapable of asking her that. There we both are, immersing ourselves in silence, with the percolator somewhere in the background, our conversations languishing around us and that blazing hot autumn out in the street, right outside the window, that blazing hot autumn, which just keeps on burning itself up.

TWENTY-TWO

IN THE HOUSE UP ABOVE THE SITE, in the house where my mother, Rose, lived, the two brothers fought.

Franck and Charles, who were like two peas in a pod, like the jelly and the mold, fought because of Rose.

Because of Rose and her diaphanous skin, her wardrobe that was sometimes too skimpy, thin, and transparent, giving Franck palpitations, Franck who rebelled over breakfast, you're not going out like that, and Rose sitting down at the breakfast table and saying, don't worry, you're the only one who's bothered by it, which is both untrue and humiliating, but Rose always gives him the same answer because sometimes she just needs her brother to scowl at her and shut up, even if there have been times, when things were particularly painful for him, when Franck collared her, holding her back by her arm, slamming her against the front door, tearing her Liberty-print dress, forcing her into something with a higher neckline, as he always said, fuck, why don't you wear stuff with a higher neckline, in a sort of epidermal desire to cover her up completely, to hide her, shroud her, and when he mistreats her slightly like that (but it's only very slightly, of course, because he could never resolve to damage her and can't bear the thought that anyone—least of all him—should hurt Rose), when he mistreats her then and because he is unhappy and confused, he keeps saying to Rose, it's you who makes me do this, it's your behavior, Franck in denial, stubborn and blind and deaf to everything Rebecca, Charles, or Rose say, even though Rebecca sides with her poor suffering son and tries to calm Rose by saying, he's not himself, when Franck does things like this, he's not himself. And she reminds Rose of the blazing sunshine of their childhood when Franck was just the sweetest boy you could find, the most attentive, the most protective boy in the world, who took care of his sister and called her a countess. Rose herself, who doesn't remember the endless summer that seems to have been her childhood according to family lore, is not always prepared to understand her brother's misdemeanors.

And on that particular day when Rebecca and Rose came home in Rebecca's old Ford, which made a noise like a pressure cooker melting, when they got out to take the shopping bags from the trunk, they noticed there were no lights on in the house, are they not here? Rose asked, and Rebecca said, I don't know, they might be sitting in the dark, which didn't make any sense, Rose couldn't imagine what her two brothers could be doing in the dark, no way they could play checkers or read the paper, and she couldn't even see the spasmodic bluish UFO glow of the TV in the kitchen, she leaned up to the window to look inside, with her boxes of breakfast cereal and sliced bread in her arms, Rebecca said, go on then, and Rose felt slightly worried but almost immediately felt irritated by her own concern, what are those two stupid-heads doing? she thought, even though she had never had any cause to call them two stupid-heads and if you had asked her about them, she would have said, my brothers, Charles and Franck, my precious brothers, because they were the ones who brought sustenance and comfort to their existence for all four of them, because they really mustn't leave anytime soon, if so, eek! nothing left to eat apart from paltry allowances and the eggs from Rebecca's depressive chickens, because her brothers were the mainstays of the household.

So when Rose went into the kitchen with her arms so full that she couldn't turn the light switch, she bumped into Franck's body in the dark, she tripped and fell headlong on the floor in a muddle of cardboard boxes and cans of beer—like ball bear-

ings rolling playfully, their euphoria addressed at no
one in particular, and disappearing under the cupboard, into corners full of spiders and grains of
orange rat poison.

Rebecca was behind Rose. She was not the sort
of woman to lose her composure, so she switched
on the light and yelled to wake Franck and Rose, in
case they had just gone to sleep suddenly like that,
rather ostentatiously, in the middle of the kitchen,
brother and sister linked together, limbs sprawled,
well, they could have, funny things do go on
between brothers and sister, things you can't talk
about, like with mothers and fathers, so Rebecca
shouted, she swore first then she shouted, what the
hell are you doing? it was only after she'd got so
angry that she noticed Rose was trying to get back
up and Franck's face was swollen, both his eyelids
purple and puffy as if he'd been stung by a horsefly,
then she squealed, almost hysterical now—because
she could also be the sort of woman who lost her
composure—we've been attacked, oh boy, oh boy,
oh boy, we've been attacked, they've taken everything and killed my son, moaning and pushing Rose
aside so that she could weep over Franck, making
quite a performance of collapsing and sobbing while
Rose stood bolt upright beside her, her hands
hanging useless without the beers that were now
scattered to the four corners of the room and

without her boxes of breakfast cereals, Rose empty-handed and confused, this woman's mad, are you sure this woman's my mother? there must be some mistake, you must have made a mistake, Rose pulling her coat closer around her, her coat with the rabbit-fur lining that was three sizes too big for her, because she could feel the cold wind coming up from the lake full of catfish, weaving through the pine trees and nudging into the kitchen, Rose saying, did Charles do all this? but Charles is so gentle and kind, I mean, what happened in this kitchen? hearing the ticktock of the plastic clock above the sink amplifying inside her, that ticktock now overriding her mother's despair and her incongruous weeping while Franck groaned as he regained consciousness, and Rebecca shook him, still screaming, you're not dead, you're not dead.

—

Franck was not dead, he was just bruised and mauve. He let Rose bandage him while their mother moaned, rocking on a stool with the regularity of a bonobo ape, and he didn't say a word. He didn't want to tell them anything about his row with Charles, Charles who had gone down to the town for help, Charles who had first knocked Franck out (to his own surprise), Charles who was so gentle and so kind, Charles who couldn't stand another word from Franck riling him about his apathy and about

135

how much freedom he gave Rose, Charles who eventually flew into a rage because Franck was implying that his indifference to Rose's behavior had nothing well-meaning about it but was actually a sign of some peculiar perversity. Charles who had eventually knocked Franck out with all the efficiency of a quiet man, terrified by his own strength and going down to find help but then forgetting, completely obliterating the bit about getting help from his mind, and ending up at the hotel by the bridge with a whore, drinking and drinking with the whore, the one and only whore in Milena who managed to be young, pretty, and ruined all at once, who had herpes and other more subtle illnesses lying in wait in the folds of her flesh, but she was such a gentle, loving whore, the sort of model whore they all dream about, tender, fragile, and not too talkative, and who—in spite of the herpes and the subtle illnesses—managed to maintain that air of faded freshness that made them want to be with her and never let anyone mistreat her again, Charles in the hotel by the bridge drinking with Anna the whore, drinking and screwing her of course, doing it standing up in room number 5, letting her leave and then carrying on drinking and saying to himself, I came to get help, I think, but why? who for? I think I dreamed about a stag beetle in a very blue summer sky, an aggressive artificial blue, draw me a summer sky, I'll paint it for you in acrylics or oils in a church-ceiling blue, a lived-in blue, and Charles feeling his head thumping and thinking, we really should have a phone up there, I wouldn't have to keep going for help when the need arises, I must have a phone put in, it doesn't make any sense being cut off from the world like that, why does mom want to cut us off from the world?...Unless it's Franck who wants us to stay hemmed in up there...Yes, it's Franck who's so frightened of the outside world...I don't give a fuck about Franck and his stuff with Rose, he'll just have to confine her, stifle her, bind her, gag her, while he's at it he can just lock her up in the wash-house and we won't mention her again, and Charles suddenly remembering what he had done to Franck, the blows he had dealt him, frowning and seriously doubting the memory of it, thinking, all this is as artificial as the blue sky with the stag beetle, no, no, I can't have hit Franck, why would I hit Franck that hard? I don't give a damn what he does to Rose, he's very welcome to stop her going out and shaking her ass to attract the rabble from the mine, I don't give a damn what he does to Rose.

TWENTY-THREE

THERE WAS THE WHOLE LONG SUMMER the year he was fifteen when Markus couldn't think of anything better to do than hang out with Gino and Leroy, when not one of them knew how to get up early in the morning to go fishing in the catfish lake any longer, when they couldn't remember the days of catching salamanders and bringing home buckets full of tadpoles, which they left swirling in the long grass to rot and dry out in the sun, it was the first summer when the fact that there were three of them no longer made them feel like a gang but rather a triplicate loneliness, waiting, Markus, Gino, and Leroy waiting to see what plans the world had for them, fretting about it, and spending their time vaguely promising themselves to get out of the place, out of Milena and its open-cut mines, secretly learning to drive in Gino's father's car—Gino was the only one of the three who had a father, not a very illustrious one, mind you, more the maudlin alcoholic type, but kind at heart, skinny as a skylark, with gold teeth and a slipped disc that kept him pinned deep in the sagging sofa and allowed the three rogues to drive around in his old turquoise Fiat, Gino's father sometimes asking them to carry him out to the car and load his angling gear into the trunk, setting off for the lake groaning because his back was plaguing him, parking his car as close to the water as possible, grabbing his rods from the back, and fishing from the driver's seat, sometimes Gino and Markus would go with him and carry him over to his folding chair, setting up the landing net on his left and the keepnet on his right (beneath the surface between the reeds with some cans of beer keeping cool in it), then they would go home to Milena and come back down toward evening to pack everything up, the rods, the landing net, and the old boy, while Gino's father told them, you're good boys, and Gino and Markus didn't answer and didn't catch each other's eye, just feeling a little sad for Gino's father.

Markus didn't talk to Gino and Leroy about girls, they discussed music and what they would do when they had lots of money, they talked of getting away and how long it was until they could get away (which they kept postponing until it was nothing more than a pleasant, relaxing topic of conversation, as weighing up the relative merits of different sauces would be for three gourmets).

Markus was the only one going back to high school in the neighboring village that September, the other two were still hovering, having abandoned their schooling but not yet old enough to work in the mine. This distinction didn't differentiate between them too much at the moment, although Markus was sometimes worried that he would lose both of them at once, and this made him glum and listless some evenings because of the energy he had expended in making two friends, in keeping them and maintaining the relationship—when he lived in a trailer and no one respected his mother. The thought of being abandoned filled Markus with panic and made him support the other two in any situation, so he was the one who helped Gino get his father from the sofa to the lakeside, just because he was there, casually there with no suspicious hint of eagerness, no servility, Markus knew to say "Mr. Gino" when he spoke to Gino's father, to be in the right place at the right time, to deceive adults with a sort of intuitive abruptness, to be charming—but not enough to make the other two jealous, just enough to make them enjoy his company—and funny.

Milena was an asphyxiating furnace all through that summer. Markus wore the same clothes as in winter, his mom saying, aren't you a bit hot? but it was impossible for him to show his forearms or calves, so he recoiled from the idea of exposing any skin, no, no, he's not too hot, actually savoring the slight smell he occasionally gave off, so slight it almost seemed to be asleep, with no aspirations to expand and spread. The three boys spent a lot of their time at the bar and on the pinball machine, and when they ran out of money, they stayed in the living room at Leroy's house in front of the TV, slumped among the cushions, their legs spread out in front of them so that Leroy's mom said, it feels like my living room's full of legs, you're taking up the whole room, but she usually felt happier knowing they were there than in the bar, so she would bring them Cokes and ashtrays and would close the door as she went out.

Markus never took either of the other two home, even though his mother sometimes suggested it, pretending not to understand—or genuinely not understanding—why he never asked anyone to eat with them, and always saying, I could drive them home afterward if it's too far and too late for them, going on about it so much that Markus ended up slamming the door of the mobile home, making the string of lights on the doorstep swing and clink furiously, Markus feeling sad, and nauseous from being so sad, unable to bear his mother any longer, with her complaints about her medication for cholesterol or high blood pressure, saying, these drugs make me gain so much weight, and when she stopped taking them, she said, ever since they took me off that one, I just eat the whole time, it makes me so hungry, always the victim of her medication or the absence of medication, so Markus would go off to see Leroy and Gino or he would decide to walk through the pine forests just to hear the pine needles snapping under his feet with that delicious sound like breaking toast, the sensation had always calmed him and given him the same satisfaction as splashing through puddles as a child.

That was how Markus, Gino, and Leroy spent that summer waiting for something to happen.

TWENTY-FOUR

MRS. ISIS TALKS IN SNIPPETS. I harvest, collate and adjust the male elements with the female, in the evenings I lay out elements of both sexes on the bedspread in the hidden bedroom—the pantry—and I concoct something, adding to the mix a pinch of everything I know about Mommy Rose and Markus, I sprinkle it, fill in its gaps, and invent bits until the whole thing stands up, I'm working very hard to make their story stand up on its own. Sometimes my efforts leave me in despair, there are too many points of support missing, my power to construct it crumbles, flickers, and goes out completely. I can't do it.

I talk to Mrs. Isis about Mr. Loyal, who still goes to his nude cabaret every day and every evening, but he is never home late, it's not his job to keep an eye on what happens during the night. Since finding out that Mr. Loyal manages that sort of place, I can't muster any enthusiasm to go to the cabaret, even secretly—which might be quite exciting. I don't want to bring the image I have of it face-to-face with what it really is. It would always be dirtier, smellier, more dilapidated than I imagine it and Mrs. Isis describes it. I tell Mrs. Isis that I find Mr. Loyal's indifference suspicious, just like his stubborn refusal to call the police to look for mom. It's because he thinks she's left him, my good friend replies. He's been thinking she would leave him for years, he can't get over the fact that such a gorgeous creature would agree to spend her life with him. Yes, she says again, he thinks she's left him.

I ponder this.

And that very evening I decide to reveal to Mr. Loyal the existence of the newspaper, of the article about my real father, the one with the stash of DNA, who tried to hang himself with a jump rope in his cell (jump rope/cell, juxtaposing those two terms has absolutely no meaning to me, I stick them together but they're not connected in any way, they drive each other apart like magnets, they've just ended up side by side on a Scrabble board, triple word score, and I can't seem to make a real sentence with them).

It is eight o'clock, we're both sprawled on the sofa (with a talk show on TV), we're not eating ice cream, it's beginning to get too cold for that, we're nibbling apple fritters, I wipe my sticky fingers on my sweater, Mr. Loyal never comments about my dubious hygiene, he never makes me wash, lets me stew in the silky sweet smell of my clothes, he doesn't say anything if I fiddle with my toes while he's eating, and if my hair is really dirty, he braids it for me. Mr. Loyal is infinitely indulgent with me.

So I launch myself and announce, I think Markus has something to do with this.

Mr. Loyal is very skilled at disguising his feelings, unless he actually has very little feeling, he just carries on licking his fingers and says, Markus? I try to work out whether he's hiding something in that "Markus?" I watch him out of the corner of my eye but he doesn't let anything show.

Who's Markus then? asks Mr. Loyal. It strikes me as indecent to tell him, Markus is my father, the proper real one, it would be like giving him a piece of bad news, like saying, the weather's going to be terrible for your boat trip tomorrow, or maybe, I think that ugly mole you've got is a malignant tumor, I look at him, he's pretending not to know anything or perhaps he really doesn't know anything—could it be that neither mom nor Mrs. Isis ever revealed my actual father's name? I'm tempted to dodge his question. I think mom knew someone called Markus, I tell him. Mr. Loyal accepts the information in an offhand way, one of her musicians? he asks, peering at his chubby fingers covered in sugar, twinkling like sequins. I sigh, how can I tell him that I'm busy piecing together an adolescence for my mom, who has disappeared, that I spend my days arranging for Mommy Rose and my father—the proper real one—to meet. I'm not feeling so sure of myself anymore, I think Markus is my real father, I tell him. I wait for the thunder and lightning but nothing happens, I close my eyes and open them again, Mr. Loyal is wriggling down into the sofa, his shirt all sticky with sugar, I think Mrs. Isis tells you too many stories, he says. Mr. Loyal gets up, whispering, you know, women who haven't had any children, sometimes, it gets too much for them. He heads off toward the kitchen, I hear the sound of the refrigerator door, its little engine starting up as if to welcome Mr. Loyal and offer him the wonders it has on display, look, sir, today we have passion fruit yogurts on the bottom shelf, and on the top shelf a selection of cheeses in punctured plastic packaging, I concentrate on this whirring from the kitchen, not moving, I'm far too stunned for that, trapped in a state of confusion, which holds me fast in the deep, soft cushions, Mr. Loyal comes back into the living room with a yogurt and a spoon and says, would you like to paint your room a different color? I can just see it in raspberry pink or lime green, what do you think? I don't want to answer, I don't want to move, I'm overwhelmed by an indefinable fear, I want to understand how everything works in my life, why everyone lies with such perfect candor, I don't know anything anymore, I suppose I'll just have to carry on assembling this puzzle with all these fucking little pieces that don't fit together, and trying to fathom the mysteries of mom's life despite Mr. Loyal's warnings.

TWENTY-FIVE

MARKUS SPOTTED ROSE IN OCTOBER and kept an eye on her comings and goings at school. The thought of seeing her motivated him to go to the shabby place every day, catching the bus in the morning mist, parking himself at the back by the window and breathing on it to make it cloud over, drawing skulls that trickled and blurred, shooting furious looks at any intruder who happened to sit in his place, evicting the intruder through sheer visual pressure, falling asleep on the way there or pretending to fall asleep, thinking about this baffling Rose, Rose who never takes the bus, who arrives on a bicycle (imagining her calves, her thighs, and the tendons of her forearms), Rose who is never cold, he has heard there is no heating at her house, that her mother or her brothers or one of her brothers—he can't really remember—is a bit crazy when it comes to anything modern and comfortable, apparently they eat eggs from their chickens and carrots from their garden, they wash in cold water out in the yard, her brothers go hunting, they smoke their own meat and distill their own liquor, Markus doesn't believe everything people say, he knows how hard it is to pass yourself off as normal when you live slightly outside the town.

In the afternoon Markus goes to the school library and positions himself not far from her, he's not really sure why she has such an effect on him, he would probably do better to go home to Milena and see Leroy and Gino, do a bit of schoolwork, screw around with them, waiting for the day one of them suddenly becomes rich or famous, he would do better not wasting his time staring at this girl who spends entire afternoons not noticing him (am I really in the same space-time as her?) and studying, maybe Rose is really just sitting there in the quiet rustlings of the library so that she can delay going home for as long as possible, knowing that Franck will always be waiting for her by the school gate anyway, standing there with his bike, holding the handlebar in his right hand, stiff as a flagpole, impermeable to jeers, Franck who just can't bear the thought of his sister going home alone, you can only imagine the feeling of respite she gets by staying for hours in the hushed atmosphere of the library, far away from Franck, her chin resting on her hand, daydreaming with that look she has perfected in her eye, a look of deep concentration, "don't disturb me," the look of a girl who is completely absorbed, screwing up her eyes slightly, defying anyone to come and interrupt her meditations.

In a week's time, I'll talk to her, Markus tells himself.

And then, in mid-November, he suddenly realizes she has stopped coming to school. He looks for her on the first day. There is a hard frost now in the mornings, the stones around the lake that have water in them split open with a loud crack, you can hear them as soon as the sun starts to come up. It will snow soon. Markus tells himself it's the winter that is stopping Rose from coming to school, that she can't bicycle any longer, or that her brother Franck—who's been lumbered with a reputation as a surly brute at the Site and in other places—won't let her go to school anymore, Markus starts worrying, he can already see himself as her savior, I'm going to climb that hill, he tells himself, I'm going to cut through the forests above the mine, and I'm going to see where it is they live, I want to get this clear in my mind, no one can stop my Rose from going out (oh my God, he's calling her "my Rose" already, Markus is lost now), a few days go by, Rose doesn't show up, Markus decides to do something about it the following Sunday.

On Saturday morning when Markus wakes up,

it isn't really morning anymore, it's something like eleven o'clock, his mother has left a note for him—loving, with gentle instructions—Markus reads the note, she's put, it's been snowing, before listing the possible meals he can concoct for himself from the refrigerator, so Markus looks up, opens the curtains, and nods to himself, it's been snowing.

This will just complicate what he has to do on Sunday but now he feels his expedition is full of daring. The thought of climbing up to Rose's house the next day to see whether someone is holding her against her will creates soft palpitations in his chest. It's as if there are bubbles bursting under his sternum.

At some point on Saturday, Markus calls Leroy and Gino, who don't seem to be feeling great, getting depressed in their respective bedrooms. They chat on the phone for a long time and decide not to move from where they are. The snow makes them feel gloomy, it's lost the exhilarating powers it had when they were children.

So Markus ends the day watching Japanese cartoons.

Markus would have liked to draw—or if not that, to have lived in—one of those animated films where girls have disproportionately large eyes with multicolored facets and a dazzling gleam in the iris, he likes their tiny noses and their willowy bodies, they are often haughty, enraged, and all-powerful, with plastic-looking hair that seems to have been immobilized in resin.

Markus has just been sitting there with the remote control in his right hand and a beer in his left. He catches the sharp smell of more snow coming in overnight, it seeps under the doors, through every gap in the mobile home, into the microscopic fissures in the ice, he puts the heating on and closes doors and windows, the smell of snow persists, wrestling with the electric heat, there is fog coming up from the lake and it too has settled inside the mobile home, laying siege to it so that the moment Markus's mother opens the door, it can go in with her, invading their cramped living space.

Markus gets up to have a look outside. The snow has started falling and he lights the string of lights around the porch and they flash on and off, making their trailer look like a great big Christmas tree. Markus rests his forehead on the window, it is cold and damp, his forehead is flashing too, I'll get epilepsy, he tells himself.

That is when he catches sight of something coming through the swirling snow. He presses his nose against the glass but it mists up and he can't see anything. The ghostly glow of the trailer is projected onto the ground a meter in front of him. The colored lights must make their home look like a party boat or a doughnut stall in all that fog. Beyond the reflected light on the snow there is complete darkness only mottled by the dancing snowflakes, like a spectral storm of miniature meteorites. And there, in that blackness that seems to eat into the light, he sees the silhouette again. It disappears and reappears, diving into the darkness and reemerging as frequently and as briefly as a drowning man giving in to exhaustion. Perhaps it's a dog, Markus thinks, or a yeti or some drunk madman who's broken down and can see the lights flickering through the snow, Markus sighs, puts on his parka—hood, acrylic fur, zipper done up—and pushes the door of the mobile home, the lights are swaying in the wind and clattering against the plastic roof like little presents rattling against each other inside a sack, Markus manages to keep the door open despite the gusts of wind, he can hear his mother's voice in his ear saying those same words she so often plagues him with: all the heat's going out, you're letting the cold in, words that always make him picture a cube filled with air, a given quantity of it and preferably hot, but it can be replaced with proportional amounts of pernicious cold air. Markus peers into the shadows, is anyone there? he yells, amazed at the sound of his own voice, which doesn't carry but seems to fall straight into a reservoir of cotton wool. The silhouette looms out again, it looks as if it is wrapped in long veils, an elf? he wonders, it trips at every footstep, Markus jumps down the three front steps, lands in the snow right up to his ankles on the path, which is supposed to be kept clear, and runs toward the gray shadow standing out against the deep black of the pine trees, he can feel his heart beating wildly at the thought of saving someone, filled with the same pleasure he would get from warming an orphaned rabbit or a lost fledgling, Markus has to pick up his knees as he runs, he's getting closer to whatever it is huddled there, he lifts the pile of cloth and recognizes Rose in a veil—what a weird dream, he thinks—wearing broken high-heel shoes—why on earth didn't she take off those implausible shoes, did she think their tiny surface area could protect her from the snow?—Markus muses about these strappy shoes but doesn't wonder for a moment what she is doing here in her fish-egg pink veils in the middle of a blizzard heralding the advent of Christmas, of red hats and jesters with bells, improvised decorations on houses and in shop windows, decorations that sometimes stay there looking old and faded until the snow melts, until as late as April in some cases—what makes them take them down eventually? They might as well leave them there, the garlands and the incantations inscribed with spray cans of artificial snow, why don't they leave them there till the next year?

Markus feels happier debating these issues than waking up. She's broken the straps and the heels, he says to himself, incredible that anyone can get their choice of shoes so wrong. He picks her up in his arms, she feels cold and heavy for someone in a dream, he thinks, he picks her up and is aware of his own chest expanding and fluttering, I'm saving her life, let me save her life, if it weren't for me, she would have frozen, he takes her back toward the light, striding through the snow and thinking that women's bodies are more dense than they look, saying to himself, I don't know how to resuscitate someone, I skipped all the life-saving lessons, first I'll get her inside where it's warm, yes, that's right, and I'll call mom, then reversing the decision, I'll get her warm but I won't call mom, she'll go crazy, she'll pitch up here with Agathe or Lucie or Marie, they'll screech and fuss in here and I won't be alone with Rose any longer, he walks on through the snow, nostrils tingling and hands burning from the cold, he climbs the steps, Rose is blue, she might die, and the string of lights clinks in the dark, Markus closes the door behind him with his shoulder and puts Rose down, she isn't blue but she is well and truly gray, such a subtle color that he thinks he can make out the complicated network of her veins, I'm going to settle into this dream, he tells himself, and I'll only come out of it when it gets dangerous, he has put her down on the bench seat, I'll only come out of it when it gets out of hand, he doesn't dare take her into his bedroom, the seat has big green and orange squares in scratchy fabric, but what's Rose doing here? Markus asks himself, noticing that she is now barefoot, not daring to go back out to find her shoes because he thinks she will disappear into thin air, now rummaging around to find a pillow and a blanket, hesitating to call Gino or Leroy, deciding against it, no, it would be a bad idea to get them involved in this weird stuff, watching Rose breathing, hiding her arms and legs under the blanket, and noticing that they look dark in places, as if she has been badly beaten.

Markus watches over Rose, not trying to work out what she was doing there in her tiny nightdress on such a cold night, he bars the route for his own questions, just watching over her, completely ignoring his fear and curiosity, watching her until she opens an eye, sees him, and curls up tight, pulling the blanket up under her chin, and Markus makes soothing gestures with both his hands, clearly hoping to prove that he doesn't have a weapon—no knife or bent piece of pipe—repeating the words, there's nothing to be afraid of, there's nothing to be afraid of, I'm going to get you something, not sure what to get for her, trying to say what an adult would say, the sort of stuff his mother would say when she wasn't behaving like a child herself, I'll make you a cup of tea, he says, I'll make you something hot, he really wants to make her a cup of tea, but it's not the sort of drink his mother likes, do you recognize me? searching through the cupboard to find an old jam jar with a sediment of ancient tea bags, I'm Markus, lighting the gas and thinking, it'll taste dusty but it'll be hot, smiling at her but she isn't smiling, starting to realize that this isn't a dream, that the sensations are too real and that time is progressing with credible slowness, she doesn't look frightened, more as if she's already angry, her body shaking frenziedly, what's the matter with her? is it the shock? all at once Markus is asking himself the right questions, about the possible attack, the possible rape, I should have called the police, then just as quickly he forgets, concentrating on recording the scene in his memory, knowing he will want to play it back on a continuous loop, going over and over the things that happened tonight.

Markus has stayed where he is, leaning against the sink and watching her scald her hands and lips on the bowl—a stupid thing that looks out of place, he must have given it to his mother when he was little, with its mawkish message, TO THE BEST MOM IN THE WORLD, which he still finds touching, because she kept the bowl, but it also irritates him, because she kept the bowl. Markus has crossed his arms but this makes him look like an old lady, so he stuffs his hands in his pockets, thinking, if mom comes home, she won't understand any of this, the roof of the mobile home makes taut clicking noises as it freezes slowly in the dark, Markus breathes in hard to pick up the dusty-cushions smell of the place, a smell mingled with vanilla—a chemical reconstitution of an approximative vanilla—and the scent his mother wears at the moment, a slightly sickly girlish scent. Rose doesn't say anything and this silence reassures Markus, who can't face (is exhausted by the very idea of) explaining his life here with his mother, with the lake and its catfish, the river and the frazil ice and the noise it makes under the surface of the water, suddenly devastated by the wretchedness of his own existence, which entails nothing but high school and his anticipated failure at high school, nothing but his profound boredom, the slow, slow way the world organizes itself, the slow, slow days, still so much time ahead of me that I don't know what to do with it, and—right there in front of Rose—Markus feels terribly demoralized at the thought of the infinite boredom of his own existence.

"Do you want us to call someone?"

She doesn't reply. She isn't getting any color back despite the scalding tea and the blanket, to the extent that he thinks, or the thought flits through his mind, it's a ghost, I've picked up Rose's ghost, then pulling himself together and shaking his head but the idea persists, she died on the road this evening and her ghost wandered through the pine forest, shivering in spite of himself at the sound of a heavy flurry of snow outside.

"Do you want us to call someone?"

But still getting no answer, as if she were deaf, as if she had lost her hearing out in the cold, the cold penetrated her eardrums and permanently damaged her inner ear.

She didn't say anything, not even something like, it's crazy living in here, she didn't say, are you a gypsy, some kind of traveler? She looked at her own arms, which were covered in blue, and she finally spoke, could you lend me some clothes? something warm to hide my arms and legs, and him, Markus, glad of an excuse to busy himself, going into his room and searching but finding only dirty crumpled clothes, sniffing his tops, pulling a face, swearing and muttering, digging out a sweater and a pair of jeans, going back to her, warning her, I can't take you home, my mom works nights, she's gone to work by car, her shaking her head, pulling on the clothes he offers her over her fuck-me evening dress, smiling a little, I'm really sorry, but not explaining anything, given that there's nothing to explain, saying, I'll go on foot, and him gesticulating with both hands as if to block her way and saying, stay here, wait till the morning, there's all kinds of creepy wild animals out there, not daring to mention the catfish that come up from the lake, monsters that can weigh up to 180 pounds, and her slightly surprised, there aren't wolves around here, Markus saying, it's five in the morning, and even as he said it, realizing somewhere in the back of his mind that his mother isn't home, that she must have been blocked in by the snow, hadn't called so as not to wake him, and had gone to stay the night with Agathe or Lucie or her man, her sometime lover who worked at the Site.

She went paler still if that was possible, now the color of something ceramic, a dead pearl, and him saying, I'll take you home, I'll take you home, we'll catch the bus that goes around the back of the lake, the first bus, which comes at about five thirty, and her agreeing to this solution, putting on a pair of his shoes, which make her feet look like Puss in Boots, saying simply, I'm not feeling great, and noticing on her way out—but not saying anything more about the fact that he lives in a trailer on breeze blocks— just noticing the string of lights, that's pretty, she says, him following her with his torch, resolving not to ask her any questions, thinking, I'd really like to have a dog, a pointer, it could come with us now in the darkness, the snow no longer falling in the strange torpor of the last hours before dawn, with just the scrunched cotton wool sound of their footsteps, the creaking snow, and the silhouettes of the fir trees ahead of them, still deathly black, the two of them walking side by side, although it would be impossible for them to touch, hands in pockets, him thinking, she's tough, convinced as he still is, in his male naïvete, that women are fragile and have no stamina, repeating to himself, there's no blood on her, saying it so often that it sets the rhythm of his walk, there's no blood on her, which means it can't have been as horrible as he imagined, and his footsteps go, no blood, no blood, with the regularity things have when whispering messages to us, he can hear it, no blood, every time he takes a step and, just as he catches sight of the bus stop, with its ghostly light in the distance behind the pine trees, she says simply, I was with some assholes, they were totally drunk, I thought it was better to open the door and get out of there before things went wrong, him relieved and grateful to her for this explanation and thinking to himself, that string of colored lights was a good idea, that's what made her come to me, feeling satisfied in his stupidity and thinking, I can think over and over this wacky night later, tomorrow perhaps, seeing the bus coming with its headlights probing the darkness and the viscous sound of snow spurting from the tires, him thinking hastily, she can't just disappear like this, she'll have to give me my clothes back sometime, reassured by this thought as she turns toward him, stands on tiptoe, kisses him on the cheek and, perhaps to balance herself, skims her hand over his, holding it for a moment, just a fraction of a second, the time it takes a second to divide itself into hundreds of pieces, but as she puts her foot on the step up to the bus, her fingers are still touching his, he feels his heart skip a beat, a precious feeling, he wants to remember the touch of her fingers at daybreak, she gets into the bus, doesn't pay her fare, sits at the back, gives him a little wave, and now Markus is all alone beneath the light at the bus stop, Markus who watches the bus leave and experiences absolute solitude lodged very precisely under his solar plexus, Markus who wonders what has just happened and hopes that Rose's appearance on that cold night will bring a definitive end to his boredom.

TWENTY-SIX

MARKUS WANDERED AROUND TOWN through the weeks leading up to Christmas, he had no desire to hang out with Gino and Leroy, to tell them how Rose suddenly appeared in the middle of the night—his story had to remain a secret, he couldn't talk about it for fear it would lose its miraculous qualities, he spooled through the scene over and over again in his head: a ghostly Rose walking through the snow with her bruises, he unwound the whole reel, choosing to freeze-frame on the little wave she gave him in the bus when she left just before dawn, deciding to read into it a promise, occasionally catching himself with a beatific smile on his face when there was absolutely nothing to be smiling about, then, as if deliberately to get a grip on himself, stumbling on the uneven ground, telling himself, I'm a stupid-head, repeating it constantly as if to cut short his natural romanticism.

Markus hung around the supermarket because it was somewhere warm and free—so long as you didn't buy anything—it was better than the trailer, better than the restaurant where his mother was a waitress, better than the library at school where Rose no longer went. And now that he was going through a phase when his mind suggested fairy-tale solutions to his situation, the buildup to Christmas comforted him with the possibility of magic in the world. Markus fingered wreaths, advent calendars, bearded elves, cinnamon biscuits, and translucent candied fruit gleaming like beads, like marbles, like polished cat's-eyes, he squelched through the molten snow on the tiled floor, stationed himself in front of shelves of food as if comparing the price of chicken joints, and steeped himself in the cloying music—electronic chimes and tinkling bells— punctuated by the hasty brayings of a salesman chuckling into his mic to attract customers to his stand of cheeses flavored with herbs. Markus pre-ferred to stay inside the supermarket rather than to go back out because of the animal-skin boots, the corduroy pants, and the embroidered hats they were all wearing outside, because of the enormous neon snowflakes and the shooting stars swinging from the streetlights. Markus preferred sulking inside the store even if no one was interested in his sullen expression—because there were a lot of people like him who seemed to get gloomy or downright scared by the advent of Christmas. Anyway, the security man had not yet seen fit to ask him what the hell he was doing there every afternoon, not buying anything but dawdling in the aisles of this grim place, jingling his keys deep in his pocket, making a constant clinking sound like small change.

Markus wasn't surprised when he saw Rose— given that that was why he was hanging around there—with her mother and Franck heading toward the back of the shop like three angry people, a family with a score to settle, who didn't want to do it in front of everyone but intended to make it very clear that something was not at all right.

Markus hid in the drinks department, he saw the three of them marching over to the meat aisle, they look like Chechen rebels, that was what Markus thought (and he had his own very clear idea of the Chechens), they look like Chechen rebels with their rabbit-skin coats, the ear flaps on their hats, and their rubber boots—boots that looked as if they were stuffed with cotton wool or scrunched-up plastic bags, Markus couldn't see very clearly, they've probably slipped serrated knives inside them, he thought, and fat revolvers in their pockets, the Chechens scattered: the mother (wan expression, dry pink skin, the exhausted look of a woman trying to raise children and chickens in a brutal climate) clinging to her cart, the brother (jaw tensed, a caricature, I'd like you to draw me an irascible teenager, a feast for anyone into physiognomy), and the sister (Rose, queen of the Chechens). They dispersed: hardware, groceries, meat. Markus thought he might head toward Rose, chance across her, bump into her, be behind her just when she needed to get a packet of biscuits from the top shelf, but he stopped himself in time, he noticed that the brother hadn't gone all the way to the hardware aisle at all, he was kneading something in his hand—the fat revolver?—and watching his sister.

Franck was there, at the end of the aisle, surrounded by all that twinkling cheerfulness, bang in front of a flashing, grinning reindeer, there he was, bent double, watching his sister, Markus couldn't get over it, the guy's crazy, he said to himself, he watched him set off down the row parallel to his sister, taking tiny footsteps, trotting along it, Markus glanced over at the mother, who had stopped dead by a freezer and seemed to be going to sleep to its refrigerated purring, the mother must be on medication, Markus thought, she looked so angry and now nothing, it's like she's turned off the lights, Markus followed the brother, he's going to jump on Rose, he told himself, he's going to attack her right here in the store, actually Markus couldn't see Rose anymore, he couldn't even check whether she was wearing his jeans and his sweater, which would certainly have made his life feel a lot sweeter, Markus really had to keep the brother in eyeshot, the latter was biting his nails as he spied on his sister, this guy is crazy, someone's got to stop him, if an old granny asks Rose for help with some tins of dog food, he could rip her stomach out, the brother still seemed to be waiting in ambush like a commando in the middle of the supermarket, Rose was apparently not aware of anything, she had her arms full of biscuits, chocolate, and coffee, I'm staking everything on this, Markus told himself as he went over to Rose, who was just weighing up the pros and cons of different honey-flavored breakfast cereals, Markus passed close by her, she turned around very slowly, she was wearing neither his jeans nor his sweater, she turned very slowly toward Markus, and that meant she had her back to her brother, she opened her eyes wide when she saw Markus, puffed up her cheeks, and winked at him, Markus then realized that she knew her brother was spying on her, Rose was not put out, she winked at Markus again and he felt as if he had been turned to stone, turned to granite, or more specifically, something made of limestone that would crumble if you so much as touched it, Markus couldn't get over it, Rose knew her brother was watching her, Markus's chest swelled, I'm going to save her, he told himself, I'm going to find a way to get her out of here, Rose started walking, she came past Markus, who hoped she would drop a tightly folded piece of paper on which she would tell him what to do, meet me at the quarry at ten o'clock tonight and let's run away, or something along those lines, but Rose didn't drop any paper, she was chewing on something as she passed him and Markus was so conscious of her presence and his longing for her, there and then, that he thought she must be able to feel it. This idea made him very uncomfortable. But Rose passed by and walked on. Markus stayed where he was, motionless, he was aware—on the right-hand side of his field of vision, way over to the right—of the brother's silhouette scuttling down to the cash registers to get the best sight line for his crazy purposes. Then Markus sighed very gently, moving as little as possible, he even stopped breathing, just trying to play dead, trapped inside that supermarket with its promises of parties and domestic pleasures.

TWENTY-SEVEN

It was on a Saturday that Mrs. Isis announced that my father and mother, Markus and Rose, never slept together. We were in the kitchen. Mrs. Isis was making pancakes for me. Mr. Loyal had gone off to his nude cabaret, to get on with matters in hand, as he always called it, I'm going out, he would say, I must get on with matters in hand, or he said, I'm going to the circus, and I played along, asking, is the lion feeling better? have the trapeze artists got chicken pox? Mr. Loyal would mumble a reply or speak distinctly but talk complete nonsense, looking me almost straight in the eye, with obvious satisfaction in telling me some fabrication that would protect me or edify me.

I spent all that time with Mrs. Isis. It was cold and gray. A very particular color, sharp and oceanic, the gray of pigeons' wings. In our part of the world the winter produces a violent wind, which hammers into the hills, snakes between the buildings, and lifts you off the ground as if you were attached to a great kite bouncing you up into the air. In winter I put on weight so that I don't fly away. I cover my rabbit hutches with big tarpaulins, I go and talk to them every day then come back down and head for the Institute, where absolutely nothing ever happens, or I manage to be not really there, closing the doors and shutters to my little hideaway, hibernating, muttering to myself, while they knock and drum on the door and unclip the hinges, but I stay there silent and steady, it doesn't worry them: I always behave like that.

When I get home, I go straight to see Mrs. Isis, and listen to what she has to tell me about mom and Markus, sitting myself next to the cooker in her kitchen—houses in our part of the world have no heating, it's cold for such a short time each year, people wear a few more clothes and huddle in their kitchens, they leave the oven door open and drink hot teas and eat lamb stew or soup, scalding concoctions that bring you out in a sweat right away, make you open your eyes wide and white, create a damp veil just above the upper lip, a little mustache of droplets, so you're suddenly very hot and feel as if you're housing a brazier in your chest.

Mrs. Isis makes treats for me, sugary, fatty, jammy, calorific, dripping, sweet treats. She can tell I'm inconsolable so she spoils me and sprinkles everything she cooks with a vaporous cloud of pow-dered sugar—a very light dusting of immaculately white sugar flying all around the room. I look at the time, it's four twenty-five, I attach particular impor-tance to the time and to the repetition of certain words, I listen to the ticktock and tell myself, I won't say "camel" today (I'm cheating a bit, it's easy not saying "camel"), I listen to the ticktock, to the noise of the gas warming our feet, exhaling its venomous breath around Mrs. Isis's small, tiled kitchen.

I tell Mrs. Isis I can remember mom kissing my thighs when I was a tiny baby. As Mrs. Isis replies, she hands me a plate—with multicolored butterflies dancing in a meadow painted by mouth by a limb-less artist—of pancakes with honey, she always spreads the honey half a centimeter thick, the pan-cake goes impossibly limp, I have to lean toward the table and nibble directly off the side of the plate, pushing it with my right hand to maneuver it into my mouth, thereby avoiding most of the mess, so while Mrs. Isis stuffs me with sweet things that will eventually block my arteries and start stockpiling themselves in my every organ, she replies, you can't possibly remember that, you were far too young.

Her comment upsets me.

I remember it perfectly well, I insist, I remember mom kissing the inside of my thighs when I was lying on my bed, I laughed and wriggled, and she said there was nothing in the world as soft as Rose's thighs, she tickled the backs of my knees and giggled with me.

Mrs. Isis sighs and says, of course, of course.

I can remember Mr. Loyal chasing me around the apartment too, I add. He pretended to be a Tyrannosaurus, and I would give these piercing screams, and laugh so much I couldn't breathe, and run away and huddle in a corner of my room, he used to shout, I can smell fresh meat, and I thought he said "fresh sweet," so I thought I smelled sickly sweet, my eyes rolled in every direction, I could feel my heart banging against my ribs, he would catch me, haul me onto his shoulder, and carry on running around with this giggling baggage of Rose.

Mrs. Isis nods.

She finds my stories boring.

So I change tack, I talk to her about Rose and Markus again because that seems to be what interests her most, I try to think of a question that might entertain her or surprise her, so I ask, when did they sleep together in the end? Mrs. Isis stops halfway through pouring a ladleful of batter into the pan to make the perfect depth and consistency of pancake. She turns toward me and looks me right in the eye, a straight line is the shortest route between two points, and she says, they never slept together.

I burst out laughing. I had a feeling she might

say that. I said, you know as well as I do that that's impossible. She digs her heels in. The skin on her neck, or rather the skin situated between her chin and her neck, starts to quiver as if someone were wriggling about inside there, a tree frog living in her goiter that has just decided to take some exercise.

My Rose, my pretty, my Cadillac, my bougainvillea (she's playing for time here), my Rose, you have to face the facts. Your father and mother never slept together.

Obviously, Mrs. Isis, I retort, and I'm a spontaneous generation, the product of God knows what kind of insemination, an in vitro fertilization, I think you're making fun of me, Mrs. Isis (she looks offended), I don't want to know exactly what they did or how often (then shocked) but I can't understand how you can be so old-fashioned or such a liar or so convinced that I'm an idiot to dare tell me such twaddle (even though the word I've chosen is quaint and almost endearing, she is hurt, she goes very red—a shocked, graceful, pinkish red—and starts shaking). So I push back my chair, stand up with slow dignity, put my napkin on the table, and leave Mrs. Isis's apartment with all the scornful elegance of an outraged countess—at least that's what I hope.

TWENTY-EIGHT

MARKUS SAW ROSE AGAIN A FEW DAYS LATER. She was at Mrs. Gerstenberg's patisserie, buying chocolates.

It was late afternoon, already dark outside. Markus was walking along the street heading for Leroy's house, where he hoped there would be a Christmas tree, garlands, perhaps even a crèche for Leroy's little sister, where his friend's mother might have made cookies and stored them methodically in a tin—as you would—so that they lasted right through January. Markus was strolling along slowly to make it quite clear to the rest of the world that all this festive frenzy had nothing to do with him. And when he passed the patisserie he noticed Franck's bicycle propped against the shop window. His first thought was, people are insane bicycling in this weather, they'll break their back or their ribs and they'll only have themselves to blame; his second thought was, that's the crazy brother's bike; the third, I can't believe that guy buys sugary crap stuffed with cream. Markus leaned toward the window to see more clearly inside the store and he saw Rose from behind, choosing chocolates in a slightly strange, offhand way with rather peremptory little waves of her right hand. Part of Markus's brain stopped functioning, he was freewheeling, he waited for her.

When she came out carrying her box—red Chinese jacket with lacing at the side and golden trees embroidered on the sleeves, slightly worn beige cord skirt, scarf knitted by Rebecca in stretched moss stitch, hat in reversed rabbit skin, rubber boots lined with, yes, with absorbent cotton—Markus told himself, I'm in love with this girl, I want to stay right beside her, and I don't want her ever to go away again.

She jumped along the sidewalk in the sanded, salted snow, she recognized him and gave him a smile that betrayed very little surprise, saying, Markus? that's weird, I was just buying you some chocolates.

And, as he gave no reply, she added, to thank you for the other night.

Markus carried on looking at her as if she were talking in a version of the film he had no subtitles for, he seemed to be trying to understand the link between this box of chocolates and his own hospitality.

I'm happy to see you, she said.

They didn't move, the puppeteers took a break, they stayed there looking at each other, him with his hands hanging limply, not knowing what to do with his limbs, her with the ribbon of the box twisted around the index finger of her right hand.

I took Franck's bike, he's at the Site, she eventually managed to state.

Markus realized that he still hadn't said anything, he no longer knew how to use his vocal cords, he was ravaged with doubt about how interesting what he had to say might be, he launched himself: are you okay? he asked gently, perhaps to make her lean forward or just to deploy his voice carefully because it felt so out of place to him.

He was quivering with excitement and had an irrepressible longing to kiss her but knew it would be impossible to do, staring at her lips—soft and dry, he speculated—taking shallow breaths of the icy air to avoid passing out, thinking so hard about the temptation to kiss her that she became inaccessible, not daring to do anything now, paralyzed, thinking, maybe I'm going to stay rooted to this spot, maybe I'll never be able to move from here again, people will walk past me outside the Gerstenberg patisserie for years and they'll say, do you remember? that was Markus, he fell in love with a girl on this very spot, so violently that he turned into a pillar of salt.

She was the one who said, we shouldn't stay here too long.

She picked up her bike, smiled at him, we need to go and warm up somewhere. She made a mysterious sign with her hand, we can eat the chocolates.

Markus felt incapable of suggesting anywhere, the possibilities spun around in his head but none of them seemed appropriate, and the longer he was silent, the more he thought, what the hell is she going to think of me? She'll think I'm a moron.

Let's go back to the trailer, she said.

He gulped.

He told himself, we'll have to stop on the way there so I can find something to smoke, so I can drink something strong, so we can get lost, so the snow can start falling again, so we can get caught in a blizzard, so her crazy brother can appear, we must somehow not actually get to the trailer, go to every bar in town, she must fall, I must fall asleep suddenly along the way, or have a heart attack, or a toxic cloud could descend on the town, or a huge fire, an attack from the North Koreans, or my mother could show up and ask for help getting her car out of the snowdrifts, I have to suggest something else.

Then Markus thought, fuck, I've never been so frightened.

So they walked around town, side by side, Rose holding her bicycle, then they went along the frozen little canal to get to the place where the mobile home was slowly dying. She talked a lot, which meant Markus didn't have to use his voice and could let himself be lulled by her words, she talked about school, her brothers, her father, the cargo of gold he had stolen, she opened doors, put all sorts of packages on the floor, he could hear her voice falling in the snow, and this sweet purring succeeded in giving him new strength, gave him the opportunity to invent brief scenarios that would get them into his bedroom, projections that he abandoned and modified as his anxiety dictated.

When he opened the door, hoping to break the key in the lock but still managing to get into the trailer, when he saw her stamping her feet on the steps, saw her taking off her hat, her scarf, her coat, her cardigan with sleeves, her cardigan without sleeves, her boots...he thought, *here* we go, I can't do anything to stop it now.

He took her in his arms and kissed her.

She seemed relieved.

They went into his bedroom and first he told her how he felt about her, this seemed crucial to him, he kept telling himself, I'm going too quickly, but it had to be like this, she had to know that he thought about her all the time, that it was this tension that made him so silent, that in different circumstances he could be very funny and talkative, which wasn't entirely true. She sat there smiling and smoking in Markus's bedroom, she took off her pantyhose and told him, I know all that. She stood up to kiss him and pushed him over to the bed.

They took some time getting undressed, each item of clothing had specific significance, it was an hour before they made love, and it was almost unbearable making love with her, because Rose must have been screwing guys since she was twelve, because he himself had made a few attempts with a couple of generous girls, because Rose had probably hung out with every lowlife from the Site (to her brother's horror), because Markus was so moved that he would have liked to be the first and for her to be the first, he was blown away and he kept thinking, what the hell is happening to me, he felt ridiculous and radiant, I'm holding Rose naked in my arms, he told himself, and it was repeated like a leitmotif hammering at his temples, I'm holding Rose naked in my arms, and even when she started talking again, about her brothers, her mother, all the crazy people who made her life impossible, when she talked about how violent Franck was, saying, I understand why my father got out of here, I'll set fire to that house one day and I swear it'll burn well with their reserves of liquor, even when she started giving details about the men she had known and about what she would like to inflict on her family, Markus just stayed there watching her and understanding her, this girl, this Rose who seemed limpid and luminous to him, he felt he could decipher the neon circuits in her glass body, all those tiny lights meant something and he would be able to read the messages glittering inside her.

It was a day of great revelations for Markus.

He looked at her, he looked at her face and thought, do I ever love this face! It was exhausting looking at her, her face was so mobile and evasive, when he looked at her eyes, he could no longer see her mouth, and when he looked at her mouth, he could no longer see her eyes, he couldn't get a clear idea of it, he never managed to get an overall view of it, in the same way that he could only feel her feet on his thighs when he also had his chin in her hair, and this dissipation of his own senses puzzled him. He would have liked her to say nothing because he found all these revelations tiring, but he also liked listening to her talking, and while he was torn between his need for silence and his desire for her to fill every corner of that enclosed, buzzing space on that snowy night, she carried on telling him the story of her father and her brothers.

Markus wasn't listening. He kept telling himself, I'm in love with this girl, how can I make sure she's mine forever (but in the vaguest of terms, his lack of vocabulary leaving blanks and gray areas), while she carried on talking, he thought to himself, I was sure I would hate someone putting their cold feet on my thighs, I was sure I would hate someone going on and on talking.

Markus abandoned himself to daydreams. Maybe she'll never be able to leave again? Markus wondered, projecting himself a few hours into the future, telling himself, we'll make room for her here, mom and me, we'll go to high school together and then I'll quit school too, I'll work at the gold mine, we'll have a bit of money, a Japanese car, oil-fired radiators, but poor Markus had already exhausted the potential for pleasure in his plans, seeing himself with her in this trailer, cut off by the snow, set in cement for decades, with screaming children, having to support his mother, a bronchial disorder, and a Rose grown fat and weary wearing a Terylene housecoat. Or he guessed she would be the sort of girl who disappeared more and more often and eventually left with the kids so they would end up thinking of him as just a sad alcoholic uncle, an obscure godfather you visit less and less. Markus shook his head to pulverize his nightmares. He sometimes even managed to make himself cry with thoughts like that, cultivating a sort of delectation for self-pity, a tendency that disgusted and delighted him.

He got his footing again and looked at Rose more closely to photograph her face properly, so he would be able to conjure it up when he was sad or lonely. He took it to pieces, labeled it, and archived it in the available filing system.

Then they made love again.

She said strange, crude things about his dick, the taste of his dick, how hard it was, its texture. He listened and found the detail she gave him shocking and delicious.

Then she put her ugly clothes back on, gently refused to let him take her home with a tiny hint of panic in her eyes (my brother will be in town), saying, I'll see you really soon anyway, and set off back down the path beneath the laden pine trees, with the bike on her right-hand side and the slow tempo of her footsteps.

TWENTY-NINE

ROSE DIDN'T REAPPEAR FOR A WEEK.

Markus lived in suspended animation that whole time. He went through every phase of anxiety and loss, she's abandoned me, her brother's killed her, she doesn't want to see me anymore, she's left town, she's very ill.

He felt feverish; he kept thinking, I don't understand, it's like there's poison running through my veins.

Then he made up his mind.

It was Christmas night, his mother had planned a meat pie and beer, along with the usual TV shows with stars who pretend to spend the holidays with you when they are really somewhere else. Markus felt it would be too difficult to bear, that he would end up huddled in his mother's arms in tears for the evening, or screaming like a madman, or running and throwing himself in the lake, digging a hole in the ice and diving into it, praying he wouldn't find the way out. He called his mother at the restaurant and told her, I have to go out, don't wait for me this evening, don't worry, I won't be home too late, he didn't give her time to object in any way, he knew that otherwise she would very quickly notice that he had spent the day drinking beer on his own, shut up in the trailer, and that his diction was beginning to go fuzzy, or at least it was very slightly halting, as if cautious, the words arranging themselves together in a rather surprising way, he hung up, put on his walking boots, his leather gloves (his mother's present the previous Christmas), his military-surplus fur-lined jacket, making sure he straightened the hood or the cold would freeze his head instantly because he had only half a centimeter of hair, and he left the trailer in the stagnant silence of that late afternoon, there was just the cawing of the crows on the edge of the lake, echoing as if the sky were a vaulted ceiling, and the occasional swish of snow falling from a tree, Markus set off in all that torpor, he could hear his footsteps crunching and—as usual—whispering mysterious little messages to him, what he heard with each step this time was *Insert coins*, and as soon as each boot sank into the snow, it happened again, *Insert coins*, it meant he could concentrate on the regularity of his stride, he could hear the murmur of his footsteps and his breathing making a hoarse slightly unhealthy sound.

Markus walked along the canal and went up the hill behind the lake, skirting around that great frozen expanse, which, even from a distance, seemed to exude damp icy air, the dismay of a drowning man, and a threat aimed at your lungs and the contorted channels of your brain, come on then, come over here then, come over with your arms full of rocks and come to my bosom, step in here and rest.

Markus climbed along under the tree line toward Rose's house. Night had fallen and he could see the lights of Milena lower down to the right, it was quite light because of the moon and the phosphorescence of the snow. Markus had never gone as far as Rose's house, he knew vaguely which direction it was in, it was the only building at the end of the track, isolated on the side of the slope, with Rose's mother's old Ford half under the barn next to the henhouses, barbed wire, and metal cans, Markus knew all that, I'm going up there to get Rose, he told himself, I'm going up there to save Rose.

The soft sound of his footsteps carried on saying, *Insert coins*, not varying for a moment, surrendering to the harmony of that Christmas night.

Markus saw the light swinging through the trees, he walked faster coming toward the clearing but still had no idea what would be the right thing to do, just sensing that Rose had to be saved.

He walked toward the first window that had a

light on inside. It was the kitchen, the meal was ready, the candles on the table lit, which struck him as a very civilized step for people he hadn't imagined would go in for that sort of nicety. There was no one there. Just that light so specific to Christmas night when you're outside and you glimpse the warmth of someone else's home through the window.

Then the mother came into the kitchen, she went over to the oven and opened it carefully, staying for a moment to see how things were going inside, she looked puzzled, she was probably thinking about something else as she crouched there, motionless in front of the gas cooker.

The first brother appeared, Charles, the eldest, the more peaceable one. He leaned back against the table and spoke to his mother, Markus couldn't hear anything, all he could do was stand there freezing on the other side of the window in a dark corner, blowing on his hands through his gloves and jogging in place to stop his feet from going numb.

That was when Franck burst into the kitchen, pulling Rose by her arm.

Markus felt himself falter, experiencing the meaning of the expression "his heart skipped a beat," very precisely aware of the following beat and the trajectory his blood made from his heart back to his heart, a violent pulsing that radiated to his limbs, Franck was holding Rose by her arm, and there was nothing tender about the gesture, he seemed—as usual—to be on the brink of terrible rage, just on the brink, teetering before submerging himself completely, so close to fury that it was difficult to distinguish his state from normal anger, Markus could see Franck's eyes bulging in their sockets as if the rest of his body were exerting excessive pressure on them, Franck was shaking Rose's arm, which didn't seem to have any effect on the mother or on Charles, both of whom had turned toward them with all the weary contempt of familiarity. As for Rose, she was letting him manhandle her as if it had nothing to do with her, shake me around, I'm not really here, I'm a long way away from you, this isn't my body, what matters is somewhere else, you can't do anything to me, except abuse my wrapping, my flesh. Markus wondered, has he already tried to sleep with her? if Franck is this jealous, is it because he dreams of getting her into his bed to rearrange the order of things? I think I'm going to scream, Markus said to himself, I have to do something. He turned away, looked at the ghostly glow of winter all around him, the black silhouette of the trees, which seemed to absorb and ingest any trace of light, I'm going to find a big stick and kill that asshole, he thought, he started pacing, torn between the urge to walk off to find a tool and his fear of missing any part of the scene unfolding in the kitchen, he took a few steps toward the barn, then came running back, the mother had taken Rose and was holding her by the shoulders while Charles was apparently trying to reason with Franck, why can't I hear anything that's being said? why does this whole business have to be so silent? I should be able to make out their cries, Franck moving closer to Rose, threateningly, Rose dodging away, extricating herself from her mother's arms, edging toward the door, opening it on the run, and ending up outside in the block of light from the kitchen, which landed squarely on the trodden snow, Markus wasn't expecting to see her appear, he felt that this whole domestic scene couldn't spill outside the boundaries of the house, what was he going to do with Rose beside him here, but he had hardly asked himself the question before she started racing over to the barn, Franck wanted to go after her but Charles checked his brother's progress, holding him back by the neck and closing the door while the younger boy yelped insanities at Rose, things to do with fucking and duplicity.

Markus ran behind Rose, he heard her rummaging about in the workshop, Rose, Rose, he said, it's me, it's Markus, her unable to make out anything but her own anger and humiliation, lighting a little lamp and turning around, seeing Markus, apparently not understanding, then saying, you came, you're here, as if everything was meant to end here, as if Markus was the conclusion to her story, looking relieved, behaving as if she wanted to laugh and sob all at once, saying, help me, Markus, I'm going to settle the score with him, turning back toward the shed, grabbing a can of gas, Markus disconnecting his thoughts and his free will, wanting only one thing, to execute Rose's wishes, telling himself I'm dreaming anyway, I'll wake up tomorrow with the radiator clicking and a strong smell of coffee, Markus taking the can from Rose and heading back to the house with her, opening the can and spilling the gas around the door and toward the cellar, just like she showed him, reassuring himself that he was merely an exemplary mechanism in Rose's hands, Rose who was now brandishing a match, one of those long matches used for lighting fires in a proper fireplace, striking it, briefly illuminating her beautiful, madwoman's face, setting light to a piece of newspaper she had found in the barn, and dropping this torch onto the line of spilled gas, both of them—him as much as her—ecstatic about the ravishing flames, the way the fire streamed toward the cellar, slipping under the door and setting light to the inside with a beatific sigh, exploding into an intense heat and now attacking the house, sparks raining down on Markus and Rose, who watched the spectacle hand in hand, a piece of flaming fabric twirling through the air, gesticulating like a ghost, and coming to rest on Rose's head, while the house burned, and her starting to scream, making a sound like an animal, a sort of hoarse moan that ran all the way up Markus's spine and burst into crackling particles inside his brain, Markus freeing Rose of the flaming fabric but, as her hair carried on burning, wrestling her to the ground to cover her head in snow, while the house burned on, and not one of its inhabitants seemed to want to come out, Markus sobering for a moment, thinking *we've killed them*, then concentrating on Rose's scalp, on her hair, which was coming away and falling on the snow, while the house burned on, her almost stunned, as if asleep, him picking her up again, moving away from the blaze and its formidable heat, while the house burned on, telling himself, they must have gone out the back, they weren't asleep, they can't have stayed in the house, and that was what he said, that same night, at the police station when he was interviewed after taking Rose there unconscious, he said, it's not possible, they can't have stayed in the house unless they really wanted to, Markus, who had abandoned his dream of running away in order to save Rose if at all possible, terrified by how unreal this all was, protecting his sweet love as he should, her with a head injury, taken to the hospital, with all sorts of extenuating circumstances as well, and him monstrously guilty, slumped on a chair, inert, thinking, this is how my life is going to stop, shaking his head like an owl, answering all the officers' questions with the words, it's not possible, while in his brain there was just this one little sentence, which would never have to accompany his escapades again, because Markus would never run anymore, or only hampered, only imprisoned, that little sentence over and over again saying, this is how my life is going to stop, while the only answer he could give the police was, it's not possible, with several different intonations and subtle variations that no officer of the law, however well-meaning, could have transcribed.

THIRTY

IT WAS CHRISTMAS EVE and I now had no way to forge any conviction, Mrs. Isis had lied too often, she had prevaricated, cut short, balked, invented, and I was the one who had forcibly extricated this possible but improbable version of my mother's adolescence, its wantonness and its gratification.

In I plunged, building up the supports for this bridge, throwing out rigging and cables, overseeing the sandbanks, observing every movement of the surrounding waters, the way they broiled and their cold shimmering. I made the whole edifice hold good and endure. I felt the need for this connection.

It was Christmas Eve.

During the day Mrs. Isis and I had made little cinnamon- and cumin-flavored cookies shaped like stars, moons, and angels—there were also trucks and kangaroos simply because Mrs. Isis had pastry-cutters in those shapes and didn't understand as clearly as I did how obligatory magic shapes were at that sacred time of year—and I had wrapped them in silver foil to hang them from the tree and watch them shining, if Mr. Loyal ever agreed to my lighting candles near the Christmas tree, given his sporadic bouts of anxiety about the place catching fire.

We had decided to spend Christmas together, the three of us, which was intended to evoke the likeness of a family but actually suggested a rather lopsided trinity. Mr. Loyal had promised to be home early. All through the day I felt trapped by my own inability to love either of them, and my worshipful adoration of my vanished mother, on and on the sky glowed, an artificial blue, they both sensed how difficult it would be spending a Christmas without mom, the sky had stayed that artificial blue, and Mrs. Isis had flitted about like a butterfly to get me to concentrate, to busy myself, to focus on something other than the thoughts that made me so gloomy. At one point I thought they were preparing a surprise for me, they had found her, she had come back, and in order to arrange the most unforgettable Christmas of my life, they had hushed up the fact and schemed so that she could reappear from a huge cardboard box tied with a big pink ribbon, bursting out of it in sequins and furs in a parody of a stag party, but that went straight out the window.

The idea titillated me despite my resistance to it, as if it were somehow lingering in my subconscious and surging up every now and then to trick my vigilance.

I tried to understand why my mother had disappeared when she heard about Markus M.'s failed suicide—who, on that December 24, I had great difficulty in referring to as my father, in spite of the nonfulfillment of their relationship, which provided it with a patina of reality—and I told myself, she's gone, all she had to do was wait for him, but all my ideas had the resonance of black-and-white melodramas, they stopped my thoughts from becoming too specific, stopped them from identifying the rather dubious links and peculiar layout of my puzzle.

I wasn't speaking to Mrs. Isis anymore. I settled for decorating our apartment on the Rue du Roi-Charles with quantities of garlands and baubles— that's me I can see there on that bright red background, all small and deformed, both a dwarf and obese, with that grimacing face distinguished by its disproportionate mouth and clowning antics.

Today will be a day without words.

It was a sort of asceticism that I imposed on myself at that point, something that was clearly connected with mourning.

Mrs. Isis didn't seem to be offended by this exercise of mine, she carried on humming and giving simple orders that I carried out diligently and silently.

Toward the end of the afternoon, Mr. Loyal came home, his pouch full of presents, which he hurriedly went and hid in his bedroom (with all the discretion of a secondary-period dinosaur), just to add to the magic of Christmas and its share of wonders.

Night didn't want to fall, the sky was still an effervescent blue. I contented myself with changing into a white voile dress, something particularly spectral, and listening to Mr. Loyal going into ecstasies over our preparations, the smell of the guinea fowl in the oven and of cinnamon and cumin permeating the apartment.

The whole thing was overplayed.

And I wondered whether I would stay till the end of the show.

It was just after that, in the kitchen, that I heard Mr. Loyal telling Mrs. Isis that one Fred—most likely some guy from the cabaret—had lost all his hair as a result of the same infection my mother had suffered from, and which had cost her her hair too. Mr. Loyal was trying to persuade the man to wear some kind of hat or hairpiece because his scalp was painful to behold. When I picked up this sentence, I was gliding along the corridor, trying to move in a particularly ghostly way (great silent strides on the tips of my toes), and stopped dead by the open kitchen door, aware—with a degree of delight, mind you—that the edifice I had cemented, crafted, and erected was falling apart.

It doesn't hang together, I told myself.

I repeated it very quietly as I slipped carefully back to my room. It doesn't hang together, it doesn't hang together, it doesn't hang together.

I sat down in my pantry bedroom, spreading my veils of voile around me on the bed, and I thought long and hard, adding up the imperfections of my original legend and listing the actual events which were modest in number—in order to put them forward as a continuous and ideal and coherent mathematical sequence.

It took me quite a long time to see clearly. Mr. Loyal and Mrs. Isis came and knocked on my bedroom door several times, but I asked them quietly to wait. Neither of them was sufficiently tactless to insist I came out of my den.

I laid it all out flat. The interrogations of the last few weeks, the infiltrations in my construction, the antipersonnel mines scattered about the place.

I started setting out my brand-new truths.

Number one, mom's head had never caught fire.

I had always accepted as fact this story of the fire because it appealed to my romantic aspirations. I wanted it to have happened like that. I was in fact still struggling against the truth. Even if there was now absolutely no doubt it was a case of raging, purulent alopecia…

Number two, Markus and mom never fucked.

I forced them to. I set up their meeting in the mobile home myself. Consequence of number two: Markus was not my father. Consequence of the consequence of number two: Markus M. probably never existed. I stared at the ceiling and faced the facts, the facts that had been undermining the foundations of my story for weeks: Markus M. was just a figure in a minor news item, a few lines in a column where they stick raw news with no frills, a name that seduced Mrs. Isis and established a foothold in her frenzied imagination.

And then in mine.

All the rest flowed from there.

Mrs. Isis was downright nuts or couldn't help dressing up the truth or inventing it, Mr. Loyal was indeed my father and mom wasn't looking for anything in that fateful paper except for a new job or an apartment she could move into with me (of course) so she could leave Mr. Loyal (I seem to remember she had already made a couple of attempts). Something along those lines. All I had done was settle myself into Mrs. Isis's fabrication.

I cried because now mom really had disappeared and my father was a fat man who was busy getting my Christmas presents ready. I suddenly felt like a prisoner in an underdeveloped country or in some part of the world where women weren't allowed to go to the movies.

I don't think I can stand it, I said out loud.

And I started thinking about old Christmases in the past with mom and Mr. Loyal, when we needed absolutely no one else, when mom sparkled in all her finery (strappy high heels, necklaces, and low-cut tops in some kind of synthetic silk), with that special smile of hers that made me think, she knows everything, she understands everything, she doesn't need us like we need her, her bangles used to clink together and you could follow her movements around the apartment by ear, she would put the radio on in every possible room to catch all the frequencies playing Christmas carols, she carried on smiling that very special smile and I followed her everywhere so as not to miss one bit of it.

I would have liked to apologize to Mr. Loyal for doubting for so long—forever, in fact—that he was my father, the one with the spunk and the dick. I would have liked to sit at his feet and kiss his toes to make him forgive me for being so bad and so crazy, but he wouldn't have understood any such signs of allegiance and reparation, he wouldn't have understood my longing for atonement, torture me, tear me limb from limb, I am tainted, spent, torpedoed.

Then I calmed down, all alone in my hidden bedroom, I stopped shaking the inside of my head like a bottle of beer about to froth up and explode, I said, my father really is my father, I told myself, we're entering a new era—something I had heard in a radio play about the discovery of America and gallant caravels setting sail—and I went off in my white veils to join in their Christmas with its guinea fowl, cinnamon- and cumin-flavored biscuits, well-chosen presents, smells, metal pendants and glass beads, bossa nova records, and butterfly earrings for Mrs. Isis, I inveigled my way into their Christmas, staying glued to Mr. Loyal all evening, him not really understanding but clearly heartened by my sudden attachment, me smiling along with them and forgiving Mrs. Isis her very old imagination, watching her sitting at the table in her appropriate dress, with her big shiny face, her ethereal blue eyelids, her doll-like cheeks, and that very particular way she has of eating creamy little niceties (the creamy little nicety giving one last sigh and collapsing between her fingers as she bites into it, the whole thing dripping lazily, leaving her fingers, lips, and cheeks sticky, but I don't find it disgusting, no, let's get that clear, I find it fascinating), I watched her, and in spite of myself, I called her Mrs. Madness, which changed to Mrs. Nuts during the course of the evening. And I spent quite a nice Christmas like that with Mrs. Nuts and Mr. Loyal, watching them and appreciating them and their smiles in a perfectly normal way.

PART THREE

THIRTY-ONE

THEY FOUND MY MOTHER'S BODY—it would be impossible, I'm sure we're all agreed, to say "mom's body"—two months later, in February, February 29, the day which skips four years.

Her body was surrounded by mind-boggling quantities of fruits and vegetables (when I heard this, I thought, they should have been counted, they should have been counted and divided into categories—fruit with seeds, fruit with stones, female fruit…The negligence of the authorities bothered me and meant that I could now focus on what was really peripheral to the event).

There was all sorts of fruit, but mostly apples, pears, mangoes, and kiwis, as well as carrots, turnips, potatoes, and big red onions.

Mom was found in a cellar in among all those plant organs. The fruits and vegetables were stored in crates or on the ground with just a sheet of newspaper to protect them from the beaten earth, they had been lined up carefully to dry, curling up in the dark, losing their water, and conserving only the perfection of their substance by transforming it into a concentrate, rather like the essence of a perfume.

The cellar was beneath the candy store.

You got to it from the outside through a trap-door in the little yard next to the store. Mom had closed the metal shutters and, just before leaving to come home, she had gone into that cellar, the trap-door had slammed shut on top of her, knocking her out, she had tumbled down the stairs and broken her neck at the bottom of the steps in among all those fruits and vegetables.

(I thought, there are loads of people who fall down stairs and come away with bruises, contusions, at worst a little fracture in some minor bone that mends without any particular care, I told myself, it's so strange, mom broke her neck, it was like falling off a bike—something banal that could transform itself into a drama, which might go for the "tragedy" option after a few moments' consideration.)

The police soon found out that the cellar belonged to a very old lady whose children had put her in a nursing home at about the time of the incident, that she kept provisions in there and allowed mom to help herself to these reserves in exchange for little favors.

No one had been into the place since mom fell face-down on the ground in there. It took until the old woman's children decided to have a look at the basement with a view to selling off their inheritance, only then could my mother's body be discovered.

I wondered whether she stayed intact thanks to all that fruit, which didn't rot, simply loading itself with sugar, drying slowly in the shadows, could she possibly have stayed as beautiful as the day she left, could her cheeks just have shriveled slightly on her perfect skull. I asked Mr. Loyal, because he was the one who had been asked to identify my mother's body, I asked him before the police took him to interrogate him in more detail because of all those lies about mom going off to spend some time with her own mother. He seemed sure of himself, which only happened very rarely, and he told me she looked as if she had just gone to sleep, as if she was having a little nap on the bare earth floor of the cellar, I felt like I could have woken her by shaking her shoulder or whispering in her ear. So I smiled at my father, Mr. Loyal, I smiled so that he knew that we would stay side by side, swimming together with steady measured strokes, so that he understood that the police would just lecture him for his thought-lessness and would marvel at how quickly he had succumbed to the despair of abandonment, I put everything into that smile, the pale glitter of my electrical filaments, a sharp courageous sweetness, I was trying to reassure him because all he had seen of me so far was my tendency to sleepwalk and do silly things, I wanted him to know, even if it was only a stuttering acknowledgment at this stage, that I had now made up my mind to walk as tall as possible—whether or not it was along some side road.

Noël Bourcier

VÉRONIQUE OVALDÉ is the author of the novels *The Sleep of Fishes, All Things Shimmering,* and *Generally I Like Men. Kick the Animal Out,* originally published as *Déloger l'animal* in France, is her fourth novel. She lives and works in Paris.